MUDDLETON

BRIAN LUFF

The Book Guild Ltd

First published in Great Britain in 2024 by
The Book Guild Ltd
Unit E2 Airfield Business Park,
Harrison Road, Market Harborough,
Leicestershire. LE16 7UL
Tel: 0116 2792299
www.bookguild.co.uk
Email: info@bookguild.co.uk
Twitter: @bookguild

Typeset in 11pt Minion Pro

Printed and bound by CPI Group (UK) Ltd, Croydon, CR0 4YY

ISBN 978 1916668 805

British Library Cataloguing in Publication Data.
A catalogue record for this book is available from the British Library.

For Georgina

Chapter One

Colossal waves crashed against the jagged rocks of the Cape, and rain thrashed down in the manicured grounds of Muddleton Crematorium.

"Who comes to a funeral dressed as a chicken?" asked Melton Thornaby.

Dr. Dreyfuss looked down at his bright yellow costume and blushed. "But Hardy always said that if anything happened to him, he wanted me to come to his funeral dressed as a chicken."

"He said that to everyone," said Thornaby.

"I know," replied Dr. Dreyfuss, "that's why I thought everyone else would be dressed as a chicken as well."

Sheltering from the driving rain, Melton Thornaby and Dr. Dreyfuss stood outside the drab chapel smoking two soggy cigarettes.

"The family tried not to take anything the Sixth Earl said too seriously," said Melton. "Marvellous chap, salt of the earth, but he was as mad as a haddock. You should know, you were his doctor."

"Actually," said Dr. Dreyfuss, "I was his dentist."

There was a flash of lightning, and a couple of drenched ravens squawked and sheltered under a hedge.

"I feel a bit of an idiot now," mumbled the dentist, his chicken suit now completely sodden.

"Don't worry about it," shrugged Thornaby, "I went to a bar mitzvah once dressed as a strawberry."

Thornaby and Dr. Dreyfuss were there for the funeral of the late Hardy Hogg-Marchmont, Sixth Earl of Hogg Earl. In ancient times they might have burned the Earl's body on a huge, blazing funeral pyre, the roar of the flames mixed with a great howling chorus of weeping – hunting dogs, war horses and a dozen or so Trojan slaves tossed onto the fire for good measure.

But this was Muddleton on a wet Tuesday afternoon, and there was to be no such pomp and circumstance for Hardy Hogg-Marchmont.

To say it was wet was something of an understatement. The sky was as black as a Blues Brother's hat, the rain horizontal. Giant waves crashed against the jagged rocks at Muddleton Point. Ancient oaks came crashing to the ground; roads were blocked; whole villages cut off. Henley-on-Thames became Henley-under-the-Thames.

Giant hailstones lashed against the stained-glass windows in the chapel, as a plain larchwood coffin was slowly carried past. Hogg-Marchmont had once attended a funeral in New Orleans where one of the pall-bearers was a midget. The chap had been unable to reach the handles on the casket, so he'd simply shuffled along sulkily, his hands shoved into his pockets. Never one to forget an engaging incident, and ever keen to enhance and improve what he witnessed, Hogg-Marchmont's Last Will and Testament had left strict instructions that there should be six pall-bearers at his own funeral, and that five of them should be midgets.

The sixth pall-bearer, the document went on, *must be a man of at least six feet, nine inches in height, who must simply walk alongside the coffin, his hand resting awkwardly on the lid.*

Above the noise of the storm, Hardy's only son Viscount Hatcher and his French wife Lady Labia Antoinette could be heard furiously copulating behind a pair of heavy purple drapes, to the rear of the congregation. Despite being eight and a half months pregnant, Lady Labia was strongly aroused by funerals, and as soon as she began to moisten, her husband was only too happy to satiate her needs. He was, after all, now the Seventh Earl of Hogg Hall, and he could do whatever he sodding well liked.

Sheet lightning illuminating the trees outside, the coffin came to a standstill at the front of the chapel, and Hardy's handsome wife Countess Isabella placed a single orchid on top of it, along with a vinyl copy of 'Green Door' by Shakin' Stevens. Isabella was helped back to her seat by her thin, frail and sad young daughter Celestia May.

Celestia May did thin, frail and sad very well. Even on a bright summer's day, when all the world was happy and smiling, Celestia May was thin, frail and sad, her face pale, and deep pools of darkness in her eyes. On an ugly day, Celestia May would cut herself; on a bad day she would starve herself; and on a good day she would go and get a tattoo.

"Who is that black man over there?" whispered one of the locals from the Pig & Pencil Case, but no one else in the church had any trouble at all recognising Lord and Lady Angus Ingleby-Barwick. He was sitting next to Celestia May and was one of the Sixth Earl's oldest and dearest friends.

Lord and Lady Angus Ingleby-Barwick was a handsome, slim and eloquent African gentleman in his mid-fifties, and he was wearing a bright, full-length, multicoloured tribal costume, with tall, matching headwear. Ingleby-Barwick had famously been born with male and female genitals – both organs furiously competing for attention in his underpants. Even Debrett's and Burke's Peerage listed him as 'Lord and Lady', and it was a purely arbitrary decision on Angus's part that his pronouns were 'he' and 'his'. Angus's father was Obateru Mantfombi Nnamdi Azikiwe – an African prince from Nairobi. His British stepmother, meanwhile, was Beatrice-Allegra Ingleby-Barwick, an aristocrat from a very old and morbidly double-barrelled English family.

At his father's insistence, Angus was sent from his home in Kenya to study mechanical engineering at university in England. He took with him his stepmother's, rather than his father's, family name, which was felt might ease his path in the sacrosanct and repulsively inbred social circles of Cambridge. Angus quickly acquired a ridiculously theatrical Oxbridge accent, perfecting the kind of vocal delivery that eased graduates into top jobs at the BBC and the Home Office, and enabled meaningful social intercourse in the watering holes of Sloan Square and Henley.

He was first dubbed Lord and Lady Ingleby-Barwick while appearing in a Footlights Revue called 'Whoops Vicar, Is That Your Dick?'. This may have been considered by some to be a cruel nickname, but it suited Angus so perfectly that it stuck like glue, even when he played Othello in his final year at Cambridge. The African did not, however, pursue a stage career, or enter the media or the civil service. Instead, he used his first-class degree in mechanical engineering to become an inventor, and already had over three hundred patents to his name. He was most renowned for his Self-Ventilating Top Hat® and his Expandable Rotating Corset®.

*

Many people had been invited to the funeral, but very few had shown up. Hardy's bookmaker was there of course, and some of the monks who delivered wine to Hogg Hall. There was also a smattering of dishevelled regulars from the Pig & Pencil Case, including the landlord and a temporary barmaid with whom Hogg-Marchmont had recently made the beast with two backs, after a gruelling session of after-hours supping in the snug.

All six members of the Muddleton Morris Men were there, in their full dancing regalia of tatter coats, breeches, bowler hats and armbands. As the coffin had passed their oldest dancer, Ben Dunn, he had ceremonially hit it with a pig's bladder on a stick.

The local amateur dramatic society was well represented. The Sixth Earl had been a keen patron of the society and had often performed in their productions. His rendition of 'If I

Were a Rich Man' in *Fiddler on the Roof* had moved many to tears, and his suitably cross-gartered Malvolio received good reviews in the *Muddleton Chronicle*. Although the *Gazette* had dared to suggest that his performance was, *like a pissed Oliver Reed, trying to do Shakespeare.*

Notable by their absence were Hardy's first wife Lady Pip Fox-Trumpton, and his second wife Marjorie Gusset, two women to whom he'd been married at the same time, and who had only met each other during Hardy's long and drawn-out trial for bigamy at the Old Bailey.

Other absentees were Tristram and Odysseus, twin sons from his marriage to Lady Pip, and Rothman, his older brother with whom he'd fallen out after a bitter argument. Neither man could now remember what the argument was about, and they hadn't spoken a word to each other since 1983.

In the second row of the chapel sat Lady Prunella and her husband Lord Patch Box-Girder. Prunella was as plain as a Manila envelope. She'd been Hardy's mistress for the past twenty years, but the pair had never consummated their rather unusual and illicit affair.

Prunella, it seemed, disliked physical contact of any kind. The more politically incorrect among us might suggest that this would make her an extremely unlikely candidate to be a mistress, but Hardy had clearly found some kind of solace in her cold and frosty countenance. Meanwhile, the Countess remained at home, missing her husband terribly and occasionally relieving her growing sexual frustration by touching herself in a special way.

Smelling strongly of damp and nicotine, Melton Thornaby and Dr. Dreyfuss came in from the rain and sat down next to the Box-Girders. Cremation is rarely a religious affair these days. It's simply the combustion, vaporisation and oxidation of a dead body in a furnace. This is usually preceded by a few flip words read by a civil celebrant who never actually met the deceased, and has somewhere far less depressing to rush off to straight afterwards.

But on that day, the eulogy was to be read by Thornaby – wine critic, adventurer and Hardy's oldest and least trusted friend. The pair had met in Her Majesty's open prison, Castle Huntly. Both had been wrongly arrested for poaching ducks and were awaiting appearances at the magistrates' court. They spent many happy evenings together drinking Australian Merlot, cleverly smuggled into the prison inside the wheelchair of Melton's elderly mother.

Had the funeral been on a Monday, this would not have been the case, because on Mondays, Thornaby was far too drunk to leave the house. But on that day of days, he was almost entirely sober – alcohol free, save for three steadying gins before breakfast and a couple of cheeky swigs from his hip flask on the way to the crematorium.

Thornaby adjusted his bow tie, buttoned his tweed waistcoat and walked slowly to the lectern, concentrating hard not to pass wind – an event which nowadays took place almost every time he moved a muscle and often resulted in soiling. He unfolded a piece of A4, lined paper from his pocket and read aloud in a deep, calm and sombre voice.

"Today we say goodbye to the youngest child of Sidney and Beatrice Hogg-Marchmont," he intoned. "The world will long remember their son Hardy, as the heir to a weighty legacy."

Accompanied by a low-level, but very distinct, squelching noise, Viscount Hatcher and his wife slipped back into the congregation and sat down near the back. The vigorous coitus was now producing mild contractions in Lady Labia's cervix, but it was more than likely a false alarm. Having said that, Hatcher's wife would have been only too delighted to upstage her deceased father-in-law by giving birth at exactly the same time as he was being incinerated.

In the front row, Countess Isabella dabbed her dazzling green eyes as Thornaby continued with her husband's eulogy. "There have been many challenges for the Hogg-Marchmont family," he said. "It can't have been at all easy for Hardy at Eton. He was a poor rugby player, an undiagnosed dyslexic and, by all accounts, a bit of an all-round arse."

An awkward titter rang out from among the mourners. Lord and Lady Ingleby-Barwick took off his spectacles and wiped them uncomfortably. Melton was well known for his gallows humour, but on this occasion, he was in severe danger of hanging himself.

"He also had the smallest ears I've ever seen," ad-libbed Melton, trying to break the ice. Hardy did indeed have extremely small ears, and from certain angles you could not see them at all. He'd once been refused admission to

8

the Groucho Club for having such small ears, and he'd seriously considered having cosmetic surgery to have them enlarged.

Melton went back to his script. "Down through the mists of years long dead, the Hogg-Marchmonts have been accused of many things," he said. "Theft, murder, blasphemy, bestiality, incest… While all of this is true, the family have always shown great dignity and fortitude in the face of overwhelming hardship and dogged pursuance by the Crown Prosecution Service."

Melton paused briefly for effect and then his cultured RADA-like tones boomed out once again, "In particular the upkeep of Hogg Hall has proved to be far more expensive than anyone could possibly have anticipated when it was built by the First Earl in the eighteenth century."

"Only this morning, I know that part of the roof fell down, killing a ginger cat, and last weekend, gaping cracks began to appear in the floor of the Great Orangery. While the Hogg-Marchmont family are aristocrats, they are not rich, and at the end of this service, I would urge you all to dig deep when the big silver plate is passed around. All money raised today will be used to temporarily prop up the ceiling in the snooker room and to fish dead pigeons out of the water tank in the attic of the East Wing."

Celestia May squeezed her mother's hand for comfort, and the Countess smiled at her daughter in a way that said, "I'm sure your father is looking down on us."

After a brief pause, Melton Thornaby continued with his eulogy for the Sixth Earl. "I first met Hardy Hogg-Marchmont at a garden party at Buckingham Palace. He had gatecrashed the event disguised as a member of the Household Cavalry and was flitting from table to table, draining half-finished wine glasses that had been discarded by the guests.

"Hardy and I shared a love of many, many things: playing cards, horse racing, greyhound racing, roulette tables... Through these shared interests, I became dear friends with Hardy, and later with his wonderful family, some of whom I see gathered here today."

Lady Labia adjusted her clingy black skirt and slid her chubby, gloved fingers onto her husband's private member, which she liked to call Monsieur Sniffles. Meanwhile, Lord Box-Girder tried to take hold of his wife's hand, but she swatted it away as though it were an unwelcome wasp. Then her eyes narrowed.

"Why is that man dressed as a chicken?" she asked her husband.

"Dentist," he said.

"We will never know," continued Melton, "if the Sixth Earl was, as he so frequently claimed, abducted by aliens in 1994, 1998 and again in 2004. It's also unclear whether he genuinely reached the summit of Everest in 1981, or whether his brief friendship with Helena Bonham Carter was indeed as platonic as he claimed.

"It was also never proved," Melton went on, "that the Sixth Earl murdered that chartered accountant in Market Harborough. Nor that he assaulted those two belly dancing teachers in Finsbury Park. We should remember him not for his high-profile trials and legal battles, but for the kind, caring, loving man that he was."

Melton Thornaby took a deep breath, swallowed hard, and he delivered the next few lines like a heavyweight voiceover for a TV commercial. "No man is perfect," he said. "Some men are more imperfect than others. Hardy may have been more imperfect than most men, but he was more perfect than many other men who were less perfect than he was." Orson Welles could not have read it better.

As if in respect for this moment, the storm outside suddenly waned, and the chapel fell perfectly still. Melton's bottom spoke quietly. The merest, gentle puff. He ignored it and continued. You could hear a pin drop.

"All through his life," Melton told the congregation, "Hardy Hogg-Marchmont had a recurring dream. He dreamt that it was a snowy Christmas morning, and that he was riding in the Muddleton Hunt. At the end of the chase, when the fox was cornered and the hounds were closing in for the kill, he would suddenly become aware that he was not a man at all but, like his prey, was a four-legged beast. But Hardy did not dream that he was a fox. He dreamt that he was a hog. A proud warthog, seated on a thoroughbred horse and dressed in a bright, scarlet fox hunter's jacket. When he awoke, he would often wonder if he was, in reality, a hog, and that his whole life was a dream. A hog's dream about being a man."

"Oh, for Christ's sake," said Hatcher under his breath. Curtains gradually closed around the coffin, which then began its final journey to the furnaces, according to the latest British Code of Cremation Practice. While this was happening, Thornaby said a few final words of farewell.

"Earl Hardy Hogg-Marchmont is going home now, guided by a heavenly light, and by the spirits of those he has cherished, adored and loved. Perhaps even now, his spirit is wondering if his whole life at Hogg Hall was a dream."

While these words were being spoken in the chapel, a tall man with a slight limp appeared behind the scenes and prepared the body for cremation. It was the seventh body he'd burnt that day. He wasn't allowed to smoke while he was doing it, but he was permitted to listen to the radio.

*

After the funeral, the mourners drove back to Hogg Hall, which was about three and a half miles north-east of Muddleton, and half a mile from the rocky coastline surrounding Muddleton Point. The house sat close to the leafy banks of the River Turd, and the north side looked out across the low hills that divided the Velch and Spurn valleys. The contours of the land in this area meant that the house and grounds had their own unique climate, and even when the weather in the surrounding area was fair, it was generally raining at Hogg Hall.

The house had been the seat of the Hogg-Marchmont family since 1793. It was set in expansive, heavily overgrown parkland and backed by wooded, rocky hills rising to heather moorland. The First Earl selected this site so that he could divert part of the river to form a large, decorative lake.

The East Wing of Hogg Hall smelt of damp and urine, and the West Wing smelt of urine and damp. The bit in the middle smelt mostly of mould and contained a collection of paintings, furniture, sculptures, books and other artefacts, few of which had any value as the majority of them were extremely poorly executed fakes – the originals having been sold to raise money for repairs to the house.

The most famous painting in the collection was 'Young Man Holding a Cock' by Jean-Antoine Piquet.

People who famously stayed at Hogg Hall included Queen Victoria, Charles Dickens and Alan Titchmarsh. The Hogg-Marchmonts also claimed that Mary Queen of Scots stayed there several times. Mary died 176 years before Hogg Hall was completed, but despite this fact, one of the apartments on the first floor was named the Queen of Scots Bedroom. It could be reached via the Titchmarsh Corridor.

Drinks and nibbles for the funeral were provided by the family's long-serving housekeeper and cook Mrs. Frapp. No one knew Nelly Frapp's age, but it was clear that she should have retired many decades ago.

"I'm only doing sandwiches," she'd told Countess Isabella earlier that morning. "If they want hot food, they can pick up a kebab or a Chinese on the way back from the funeral."

"Don't worry," Isabella assured her, "I'm sure no one will ask for hot food."

"Where's the hot food?" said Melton Thornaby, his purple snout twitching greedily. "I'm starving."

Countess Isabella ignored him. She had never been able to stand the man and wished that he'd die as well.

The Great Library at Hogg Hall was generally used for important functions. Everything at Hogg Hall was called the Great Something. The Great Bathroom, the Great Utility Room, the Great En-Suite Bathroom...

However, the Great Library was genuinely the grandest and most impressive room in the house. It had a sea view and much of the ornate, decorative plaster was adorned with wafer-thin gold leaf, large sections of it now peeling off. There was a magnificent marble fireplace, with carvings of woodland sprites, bunches of grapes and roasting piglets. The room leaked badly when it rained and usually featured a plastic bucket in the middle of the nineteenth-century Persian rug.

A log fire crackled and popped in the grate, and playing quietly, via a pair of cleverly concealed speakers, was 'Cantata No.208, *Sheep May Safely Graze*'. Isabella found this piece very calming, but everyone else in the room was finding it a bit depressing. A man from the village asked Hatcher if they had any Abba.

"Not so much as a warm crumpet?" Thornaby whispered to Lord and Lady Ingleby-Barwick, who was still resplendent in his gleeful tribal gown.

"Fear not," he replied, "I happen to have procured the keys to Hardy's wine cellar, and I'm about to poodle down there and pop a cork or two. Fancy a scoop?"

"I like the way you do business," slobbered Thornaby, and the pair slipped from the room like a couple of guilty Year 10s heading to the rear of the bike sheds to polish their trouser rifles and share an Embassy No.6.

*

Meanwhile, in the library, the family's appropriately hunched manservant Quinn O'Donnell was passing among the guests, with a tray of curled and crumpled sandwiches.

"What is in the sandwiches?" enquired Lady Labia Antoinette.

"Egg," replied the servant.

"Who laid the egg? The dentist?" giggled Labia. Dr. Dreyfuss could take it no more and quickly excused himself from the proceedings. It was the last time he would ever go to a funeral in fancy dress.

"You must excuse my wife, she is with child," said Hatcher, laying his hand on Lady Labia's considerable bulge. While his palm rested there, the baby kicked out violently and, disgusted by this occurrence, Hatcher snatched his hand away.

O'Donnell held out a plate for the Countess. "Sandwich, milady?"

"No thank you, O'Donnell," replied Isabella, her cheeks a little flushed and freshly damp from crying, "I really couldn't eat a thing. But do thank Mrs. Frapp for all her hard work."

"I shall," replied O'Donnell, knowing that even making eleven sandwiches and a pot of tea had exhausted poor Nelly to the point of collapse. She was now having a lie-down on the kitchen floor – two ammonia ampules thrust into her nostrils in an attempt to summon up enough energy to go upstairs to bed.

Hospitality was not what it was at Hogg Hall. In the old days, honoured guests were served with mouth-watering home-grown honey, freshly taken from Hogg Hall's world-famous Great Hive. Three generations of skilled beekeepers had tended the hive, until Lady Celestia May was stung in 2011 and almost died from a severe allergic reaction. As a result of this incident, Countess Isabella ordered the hive to be set alight, and it was assumed that the bees had perished in the fire. This was far from the truth. In fact, amid all the smoke, flames and confusion, the bees had performed a well-practised fire drill and escaped. Two days later, all thirty thousand of them were discovered by Mr. O'Donnell living in the feather mattress in his bedroom. The servant was awakened at 6am by an alarming droning sound, and not really knowing what else to do, he drove into town and purchased a beehive. As soon as he installed it under his bed, the bees moved in, and their vast colony had been secretly living there ever since.

In the privacy of his room, O'Donnell dined on fresh honey every morning, and he was never stung once – the creatures seeming to know instinctively that he had saved their lives. As far as he knew, he was the only man in the world with a beehive under his bed, and he found the buzzing quite comforting when he was trying to get to sleep.

Coincidentally, one of the bees had also died that day. There'd been a fight between a worker bee and a particularly mouthy drone.

"Leave it, it's not worth it!" the other bees had shouted as the scuffle escalated, but the worker took no notice, and the drone was gruesomely dispatched by his opponent. Two undertaker bees quickly removed the deceased by manhandling its crumpled carcass to the entrance of the hive. Then the body was airlifted by four forager bees, out through the bedroom window and across the north courtyard, before being dropped unceremoniously into the lake. We shall hear more about O'Donnell's bees in due course.

Down in the wine cellar, Lord and Lady Ingleby-Barwick slowly and ceremonially removed the cork from a dust-covered bottle of Michel Laroche 2005 Shiraz, and poured two jumbo-sized glasses for himself and Melton Thornaby.

Melton raised his glass. "Here's to Hogg-Marchmont," he boomed, then he took a healthy slug and perched his glass on the convenient little shelf at the top of his enormous stomach.

"Who'd have thought old trout face would meet his maker by falling off a horse," he said. "I had him down for liver failure or a heart attack."

"My money was on a stroke," grimaced the African.

"Excellent bet," laughed Thornaby.

"No dear, my money was *literally* on a stroke," explained Angus. "William Hill took the bet in 2004."

"Well, I'll be buggered," exclaimed Melton. "What price did they give you?"

"I think it was 8-1," said Ingleby-Barwick, checking in his little black book. Like many African princes, Angus's father in Kenya had owned several racehorses, and the boy had grown up in the hazardous world of sub-Saharan gambling. He used to frequent what were known as 'gambling dens', which were unregulated, and where children could also place bets. He won his first wager at the age of seven, and he had never looked back.

"Well, you've lost that," said Thornaby, taking another swig of Shiraz and immediately topping up his glass.

"How do we know he didn't have a stroke somewhere between leaving the horse and hitting the ground?" puzzled Angus.

"What did the inquest say?" asked Melton.

"There was no inquest," shrugged Ingleby-Barwick. "Bit fishy if you ask me."

In the library, Countess Isabella was sat in a quiet corner being comforted by Lady Prunella – the last person in the world she actually wanted to be anywhere near. But the Countess was always painfully polite in these situations. She'd known about her husband's affair with Lady Box-Girder for about ten years and had chosen not to raise it in polite company. Isabella's son, Viscount Hatcher, had other ideas.

"You've got a damned cheek showing your face at Father's funeral," he snapped, his cold eyes flashing, his large lower jaw twitching like the rear leg of a sleeping dog. "You're not welcome at Hogg Hall."

"I will be the judge of who is welcome in this house," the Countess told her son.

"You seem to have forgotten, Mother," said Hatcher, "that I am now the Seventh Earl."

"Go to your room," snapped the Countess. She had not spoken to her son like that since he was eight. Hatcher used his congenital underbite to chomp on his top lip, then he and his wife flounced out of the library, slamming the tall, panelled doors behind them. A moment later, he came back into the room, picked up his hat from the table and flounced back out again.

Three days later, Celestia May accompanied her mother to the crematorium, and they collected Hogg-Marchmont's ashes, which were to be scattered near the lake at Hogg Hall. The urn was a lot bigger and heavier than the Countess had expected.

"Heavens, this weighs a ton!" Isabella said to the undertaker, Mr. Mosely. "Are you sure this is only Hardy in here?"

"Many people imagine that the human body becomes little more than a small handful of ash after cremation," explained Mosely, "but this is far from the truth. The weight can vary from three pounds all the way up to ten pounds, depending on the size and density of the deceased's bones."

This was already too much information, but the undertaker went on, "Organ tissue, fat and fluids burn away completely during cremation, leaving only bones behind when the incineration's completed. So, the weight of the ashes depends on how heavy the Sixth Earl's bones were. Was he a big-boned man?"

The Countess chose to ignore the question, considering it impudent. "Well, there must be at least twenty pounds of ashes here," she said, "I'm not scattering all that by the lake, it'll make an awful mess."

Celestia May had an idea. "Can you just let us have a few spoonfuls?" she asked.

"Teaspoons or tablespoons?" asked the undertaker.

"I'm not sure," said Isabella. "What do you think, Celestia May?"

"I'd say around six level tablespoons would probably be about the right amount for scattering," her daughter replied. Celestia May knew about these sorts of things. She was a white witch and had scattered many ashes in her time.

"We have some little Tupperware containers for that very purpose," said Mosely. He went away and, a few moments later, came back with a small plastic tub. "Is this what you had in mind?" he asked.

"Yes, that's lovely," replied the Countess. "Do you want the container back?"

"Only if you're passing," smiled Mosely.

"I wonder what they'll do with the rest of Father," Celestia May pondered, as the pair drove back to Hogg Hall in Hardy's dented Daimler.

"Probably put him on the roses," said the Countess.

*

Next morning, there was sullen silence as O'Donnell served breakfast to the family. At the long oak table in the Great Dining Room, Melton Thornaby sat next to Lord and Lady Ingleby-Barwick, now dressed in a short-sleeved, patterned beach shirt and Bermuda shorts. The pair had invited themselves to sleep over at Hogg Hall, following their excessive night raid on the Sixth Earl's wine cellar.

"I could eat a horse," blurted Thornaby suddenly, his cheeks ruddy and swollen with inebriate.

"Oh God, are you still here?" replied Hatcher. "We rather hoped that you and the African Queen had drunk yourselves to death."

"Manners, Hatcher!" yelled the Countess.

Isabella was sat at the head of the table, in a chair that had always been reserved for her husband. It was a magnificent piece of furniture, almost a throne, with a long, ornate back and two large sows' heads carved into the walnut armrests.

"Shouldn't my husband be sitting in that chair?" sneered Lady Labia, as she daintily transferred a devilled kidney from plate to mouth. The baby kicked her, and Viscount Hatcher fidgeted uncomfortably. As much as he was desperate to take up the role of Seventh Earl, he did not really want to lock horns with his mother again that morning. Better to let a little more of his father's dust settle first.

"I think we should leave the chair empty," whispered Celestia May, as she sipped her caffeine-free tea. "Father would be furious if he knew someone was sitting in his place."

O'Donnell placed a plate of button mushrooms and scrambled egg in front of the Countess, but she politely pushed it away.

"I couldn't bear to look at an empty chair," she said. "I still haven't really come to terms with Hardy's death."

Isabella turned her head and looked towards the heavy oak door that led into the Great Dining Room. "I still keep expecting him to walk into the room," she said.

At that exact moment, the door swung open, and a man walked into the Great Dining Room. It was Hardy Hogg-Marchmont, Sixth Earl of Hogg Hall.

Chapter Two

Built into the wall, above the front door of Hogg Hall, was the Great Astronomical Clock. The clock was twenty feet in diameter with three separate copper dials revolving at different speeds in opposite directions. If the Sixth Earl looked at it for too long, it always made him feel dizzy, and sight of the device often gave him a nosebleed. The clock displayed the date, the month, the position of the sun in the ecliptic, the phases of the moon and the twelve signs of the zodiac. It also showed when the apples needed picking in the orchard, the menstrual cycles of the female inhabitants of the house, and when the River Turd would be at its highest point. In fact, the clock told you everything except what time it was.

O'Donnell looked at his pocket watch. It was 10.06am at Hogg Hall, and having attended her husband's funeral the day before, Countess Isabella was naturally a little surprised when he walked into the Great Dining Room.

"Good morning," said the Sixth Earl.

Melton Thornaby went to the toilet in his trousers. Number ones and number twos at the same time. No one said anything for at least two minutes. They'd all been through so much with Hogg-Marchmont that even this unexpected return from the grave seemed almost routine. The family simply stared at Hardy, their mouths hanging open, their eyes slowly blinking, the aroma of Melton's anal episode slowly filling the room.

First to break the silence was O'Donnell, who respectfully bowed his head before speaking, "Will sir be joining the family for breakfast?"

"Yes, thank you, O'Donnell. I will," said Hardy.

"I'll lay an extra place," said the servant, and he headed off towards the kitchen.

Countess Isabella grew suddenly very pale. She gently rose from the Earl's seat at the head of the table and went and sat in her usual place. She arranged the cutlery in front of her and put her hands on the table to stop them from shaking.

Ingleby-Barwick jumped up, ran over to Hogg-Marchmont, grasped his face in both hands and gave him a great, big wet kiss on the mouth.

"You old cunt!" he exclaimed.

Viscount Hatcher and his wife simply stared at each other, disbelief and disappointment etched deep into their faces. Lady Labia had a deep mistrust of the English aristocracy, and she actually wasn't in the least bit surprised at this turn of events. She felt a mild contraction in her womb and placed her hand on her stomach. "Stop that!" she said to the unborn aristocrat.

Countess Isabella finally spoke to Hardy, "I assume that you are going to offer your family some kind of explanation," she said.

"All in good time," said Hogg-Marchmont, and he kissed his wife on the forehead.

The Countess grabbed him around the waist and clung onto him as though she had no intention of ever letting him go. Then she suddenly released her grip and stood up, slapping her husband's face with such force she sent him flying backwards across the room. Blood trickling from the corner of his mouth, Hardy moved back towards his wife, but she held up her hand like an NYC traffic cop. "Don't touch me!" she said, and then she strode from the room with as much dignity as she could muster.

The Sixth Earl sat down at the head of the table and twirled the long hairs on his face. Like all the Hogg-Marchmonts, Hardy couldn't grow sideburns or a beard but had unnaturally long hairs on his cheeks. He ran his hands over the carving on the arms of his chair, and he hoped that no one in the room had noticed that he had an erection.

"Who did we burn?" asked Hatcher, his ancestral cheek hairs twitching with rage.

"I don't know," replied the Sixth Earl. "I didn't ask too many questions. I just paid a man with a van to arrange everything."

"A man with a van?" screamed Lady Labia. "Is it now possible to fake one's own death simply by hiring a man with a van?"

"Actually, he didn't use the van," said Hardy. "He arranged the whole thing on the internet."

"I assume this is about life insurance," said Melton, always a master of stating the bleeding obvious.

"Well how else are we going to keep this place from falling down?" replied Hogg-Marchmont, grabbing a piece of burnt toast from the toast rack and then immediately putting it back.

"But everyone in Muddleton believes you're dead," said Hatcher. "You can't just hide indoors for the rest of your life."

"Nonsense," said his father. "After a few days, everyone will simply have forgotten that I died at all. No one round here pays any real attention to anything."

"People do not forget who is alive and who is dead," insisted Lady Labia.

"OK," said Hardy, "Lady Clemency Trott-Clemence. Alive or dead?"

"Alive," buzzed in Hatcher.

"Wrong," corrected Hogg-Marchmont. "We went to her funeral five years ago."

"Are you sure?" asked his son.

"Positive," said the Sixth Earl. "She died at the age of ninety-four from a rare beak and feather disease that she contracted from her pet cockatoo."

"Oh, now I remember," said Hatcher.

"Lord Beaver-Santander? Dead or alive?" asked Hardy.

"He is dead," said Lady Labia.

"Alive," grinned the Sixth Earl. "He was only here last week playing bridge with the Countess. He has a patch over one eye."

"Oh *merde*," said Lady Labia.

"You see," said Hardy, "no one cares if one is dead or alive. I might pop into the Pig & Pencil Case this evening and see if anyone even notices me."

Celestia May spoke at last, "Daddy, where have you actually been for the past two weeks?"

Hardy smiled. "Skegness," he said.

Melton Thornaby shifted back and forth in his faeces-filled corduroys. "But the horse, the fall, the ambulance, the doctors…" he said.

"I can't tell you any more," said Hogg-Marchmont. "The less you know the better. All that matters is that when the insurance money arrives, we can prop this place up for a few more years."

Hardy was always coming up with schemes like this. He once went missing for three months in the Gobi Desert, hoping that his wife would eventually give up hope, report him dead and claim on the insurance. Unfortunately, during the exact same ninety days, the Countess also disappeared, and no one reported either of them missing. The pair both returned home on the same day, slightly embarrassed and wishing they'd co-ordinated their efforts more carefully.

The door to the Great Dining Room slammed open, and a nineteenth-century painting of a kitten in a wedding dress fell off the wall. Countess Isabella stood framed in the doorway, her face flushed, her teeth gritted. In her right hand was an envelope and in her left hand a letter. She placed the document on the breakfast table in front of the Sixth Earl, and he took a few moments to read it.

"Oh, fudge!" said Hardy.

"What's that, old man?" asked Melton.

Hardy said nothing.

"Go on, tell them," said the Countess. "Tell your brainless, lettuce-headed friends that you're smart enough to fake your own death but not clever enough to check to see if the life insurance policy is paid up before you do it!"

O'Donnell came into the room with a plate of eggs and bacon and put it down in front of Hogg-Marchmont.

"Red sauce or brown, sir?" asked the servant.

"Red, I think," answered the Sixth Earl, and he dipped a piece of bacon into his egg yolk.

"You idiot!" yelled Hatcher.

"Don't speak to your father like that!" hissed Isabella, as O'Donnell placed a silver vessel of Heinz Ketchup, and a tiny silver spoon, in front of his master.

Hatcher continued with his rant, "This was your best chance to save Hogg Hall, and you buggered it up. Just like you bugger up everything. Jesus H. Christmas on a stick, Father, you're a complete addle brain! You can't even be trusted to die properly! What are you going to do now?"

Hogg-Marchmont put a dollop of sauce on his plate and looked at his son. "I tell you what I'm going to do, my boy. I'm going to finish my breakfast."

Hatcher laughed. "Then what?" he asked.

"Then," said Hogg-Marchmont, "I'm going fishing!"

Things often went hopelessly wrong at Hogg Hall, and when they did, Earl Hardy Hogg-Marchmont would invariably go fishing. But fishing at Hogg Hall was unlike fishing anywhere else. It was a bizarre, brutal and often dangerous ritual. First, Hardy would instruct O'Donnell to prepare the lake, and the old servant would ride his bicycle down to the river. Turning a huge, rusty handle, he would open the Great Sluice Gates, and the water level in the lake would slowly drop as it drained away into the river. Fine metal grills would prevent the trout from being swept downstream, and when the water was little more than a few inches deep, Hogg-Marchmont and his companions would put on their wellington boots, wade out into the centre of the lake and kill as many of the flailing, stranded fish as they could by beating them about the heads with cricket bats. But first, they would get drunk. Thoroughly, excessively, irresponsibly drunk.

The Sixth Earl strode across the north lawn towards the lake, accompanied by Melton Thornaby and Lord and Lady Ingleby-Barwick. Thornaby led the way, pushing a stolen Tesco trolley which was laden with boxes of beer, mixed crates of wine and clinking, clanking plastic bags full of spirits.

Ingleby-Barwick struggled along behind, a kitbag full of cricket bats clasped precariously in his bony arms. One of Hogg-Marchmont's favourite old bats was in the bag. He'd owned it since he was at Eton, and it had been repaired with sticky tape many times. The bat was signed by Ian Botham and Geoffrey Boycott, but Hardy had never used it for playing cricket. This was his fishing bat. Being the youngest at fifty-nine, Hogg-Marchmont carried the heaviest and most valuable bag. The one with the cocaine in it.

Ingleby-Barwick loved these little expeditions with his old friend Hardy, and he relished the opportunity to exchange anecdotes about the pair's glory days.

"I am reminded of an occasion," Ingleby-Barwick intoned, "many moons ago, when Hardy and I were on a hunting trip on my father's ancestral land in Kenya. Those were simpler times. In those days you could kill a tiger, a lion, a rhino or an elephant without being criticised and harangued by a bunch of do-gooding, long-haired, vegetarian trolls."

"Hear, hear!" Melton agreed.

Ingleby-Barwick continued. "Hardy shot many elephants in his day and now here he was again, standing on the roof of a Land Rover, his huge H&H Magnum rifle aimed directly at the forehead of the largest elephant you've ever seen. It was a female. She was old, and tired, and she was standing only a few yards away from us. The beast knew that her time had come. She stood quite calmly, quietly making peace with her maker and readying herself to go to that great, steaming pool of mud in the sky. She closed her eyes and prepared to receive Hogg-Marchmont's bullet.

"'It's no good,' Hardy said suddenly, 'I can't do it.' The beast slowly opened her eyes. Hardy turned to me and smiled. 'Angus old chap,' he said, 'you and I have known each other for many years, and I know for a fact that you've never managed to bag an elephant. This one's all yours.' He handed me the gun, and without a moment's hesitation, I blasted the bugger's brains out!"

*

As Hardy, Melton and Ingleby-Barwick reached the edge of the lake, the water level was already falling. Within a couple of hours, it would be low enough for battle to commence, so there would be plenty of time for what Melton Thornaby liked to call a Liquid Picnic.

Thornaby unpacked the wine first, and while the others were pulling on their wellies, he poured three large glasses of Napa Valley 2008 Cabernet Sauvignon. This wine is normally around £150 a bottle, but Melton had slipped this particular bottle into the pocket of his overcoat while covering a wine tasting at Harrods for the *Daily Telegraph*.

Lord and Lady Ingleby-Barwick raised his glass and proposed a toast. "To life after death!" he announced, and the three men downed their plonk in a single gulp. Meanwhile, O'Donnell strained every muscle in his old body to turn the handle of the Great Sluice Gates on the far side of the lake.

Melton took a swipe at a plump bee that seemed to be taking an unhealthy interest in the dregs at the bottom of his glass.

"Bloody pests," he said, "I thought we'd got rid of those buggers years ago."

The plump bee, whose name was Arvid, spiralled upwards and joined his foraging co-worker Egil, who had already banked southwards above the lake and was on his way back towards Hogg Hall.

"I hear the queen's pregnant," said Arvid.

"Who's the father?" replied Egil.

The pair swooped in through O'Donnell's bedroom window and disappeared into the beehive under his bed. Queen bees only have sex once in their lifetime, but during this singular act of congress, they receive enough sperm to fertilise two thousand eggs per day for five years. Which is a horrible thought.

Two house bees appeared and helped the foragers unload. The pair had a healthy haul of nectar and pollen. Arvid held on firmly to the walls of the hive while the house bees licked the pollen from his hairy back legs, a process that usually took about three days and that Arvid thoroughly enjoyed. House bees are always eager to help unload the foraging bees that bring in the pollen, as they secretly wish they were foraging bees too, and they love to hear little stories about the outside world.

"What's the weather like outside?" asked one of the house bees.

Egil spun around and gave the skunk eye to his leg licker. "Just button it and get that gunk off my legs!" he said.

Back at the lake, the bottle of Napa Valley was gone within minutes. Melton Thornaby loved Californian reds. He also loved French reds, Spanish reds, Chilean reds and South African reds. Any red at all, in fact, as long as it wasn't Italian.

Melton's hatred for Italians all stemmed from a bad experience he'd had with a raven-haired grape picker in Northern Tuscany. He'd fallen head over heels in love with the woman, and the pair had enjoyed a short but passionate affair. Melton returned to England, and six weeks later, he plucked up the courage to telephone the woman and propose marriage. To his surprise, she told him that the affair was over, and when he asked why, she explained that a month after he left, she had found a condom inside her vagina. Melton desperately tried to explain that he had never used a condom in his life, but it was too late. He'd lost the love of his life forever.

Next to be opened was a rare 1999 Howell Mountain Cabernet Sauvignon at around £130. Melton had been saving this for a special occasion and he could think of no more important event than celebrating the death and resurrection of his oldest friend. Vivid, nuanced and well structured, the wine had a softer approach than the Napa

Valley and definitely benefited from being laid down for the past seventeen years.

"I dare you to drink the whole bottle in one go," goaded Hogg-Marchmont, and Thornaby was so caught up in the excitement of the day, that he rather unwisely attempted it. Two thirds of the way through the bottle, he lost his rhythm and was forced to projectile vomit the whole lot over Ingleby-Barwick's wellingtons.

About two hours later, the group felt they were drunk enough to go fishing. An orange sun was starting to dip behind the moorlands, and the water in the lake had settled at just the right depth – not so shallow that it might completely ground the trout and yet not so deep that the fish were too difficult to thwack. O'Donnell was an artist when it came to the sluice gates.

Lord and Lady Ingleby-Barwick went first. The sport was not just about how many helpless fish you could dispatch, but like a bullfight, it was about the finesse and elegance with which the slaughter took place. Angus caught sight of a semi-grounded trout and carefully slid his cricket bat underneath it. With the skill that only comes from many years of practice, he flicked the trout out of the water. It rose high into the air, and as it came down, he swung his bat and hit the fish for six.

"Well played, sir," applauded Melton Thornaby, and he splashed towards shallower water. Melton's technique was a lot more direct. Spying an almost motionless and half-dead trout, he smashed its head in, with a single blow.

Ingleby-Barwick was enjoying himself. This was beginning to remind him of his hunting trips with his father at Saiwa Swamp in the Rift Valley. Of course, in those days, they would have been accompanied by at least a dozen servants, who would carry and load their guns and keep them topped up with boozy Dawa cocktails.

Angus spied two trout trying to swim in the deathly shallows near the Great Ornamental Bridge, and he crept through the water, making as little sound as possible. He deftly flipped the first trout out of the lake, and while it was still in the air above him, he flicked the second trout upwards. Then he span elegantly around on his own axis and batted both fish, one after the other, high into the trees.

"Bravo!" cried Hogg-Marchmont, and he went looking for a fish of his own. About ten feet away, a handsome rainbow trout poked up its head. It had found a small area of deeper water and was one of the few fish in the lake that still had enough depth to swim. Hardy moved gently towards it, his boots slowly filling up as they got out of their depth. He raised his bat, as if awaiting a fast delivery from Flintoff at The Oval. As the trout swam closer, he thrashed out, making a huge splash, but missing the fish by several feet. Furious, the Sixth Earl reached into his jacket pocket, pulled out a pistol and shot the creature dead.

"Bad show!" cried Melton.

"Oh dear, oh dear, that really isn't cricket at all," insisted Ingleby-Barwick. "I'm going to have to confiscate that weapon, you wicked boy."

"It's a fair cop," growled Hogg-Marchmont, and he tossed the handgun towards the African. In trying to catch it, he accidentally pulled the trigger and the weapon discharged, narrowly missing Thornaby and simultaneously removing the corks from two of the wine bottles on the bank.

"Nice shooting!" applauded Hogg-Marchmont. At that point, the weapon slipped out of Angus's hand and fell into the water. He fished it out, and to see if it was still working, pointed it at Hogg-Marchmont and pulled the trigger. The gun misfired with a harmless click. Bored, he threw it onto the bank and once again began thrashing away at the trout with his cricket bat.

The Hogg-Marchmont family had a long history of alcoholism. The Second Earl drank twelve bottles of wine a day and yet still seemed to continue to function adequately. He was a passionate traveller, builder, gardener and art collector who transformed Hogg Hall. He inherited the title in 1811, along with twelve other major estates covering a total of 850,000 acres. This made him one of the richest men in England. It was the Second Earl who added the now famous ninety-nine pig gargoyles which adorned the entire length of the north facade. The creatures were intended to ward off evil spirits and bring good luck to Hogg Hall, but history tells that this was sadly not the case. He also built the Great Folly, an imposing tower on the north-west corner of the lake. It was seventy-five feet tall and could be seen from the village on a clear day. Topped with a turret, this cylindrical edifice contained many rooms for entertaining, including the Fingering Room, the Fisting Room and the Earl's notorious Circular Bedroom. It also housed the splendid, velvet-lined Great Card Room. The Second Earl loved to play cards, but he wasn't particularly good at it. It took just six months for him to lose all of his property with the exception of Hogg Hall.

Like most of England's country houses, the house was put to institutional use during the Second World War. The

West Wing was converted into barracks by the Fourth Earl, and a large anti-aircraft gun was set up on the croquet lawn. Unfortunately, condensation from the breath of over six hundred sleeping soldiers caused thick green fungus to grow on the walls, and as a result, the Fourth Earl had no choice but to evict the troops. This made him extremely unpopular with Winston Churchill, who also disliked him because he was both a confessed fascist and a homosexual. He was forced to switch sides and join the Luftwaffe, and he flew with great bravery during the Battle of Britain. His Messerschmitt 109 was shot down over the White Cliffs of Dover.

The Fourth Earl's untimely demise led to death duties being charged at eighty per cent on the entire Hogg Hall estate. The amount due was £12 million. The family's accountants proposed converting the house into a museum and safari park. Instead, the Fifth Earl resolved to retain his family home if he could, and he sold many valuable works of art. But it wasn't enough.

In the mid-1950s, the Fifth Earl drank a bottle of brandy, then took a double-barrelled shotgun and held up the post office in Lower Muddleton. He went on the run for sixteen weeks but was finally apprehended by the police, charged with armed robbery and sentenced to ten years in prison.

Hardy Hogg-Marchmont inherited the title when, at the age of seventy, the Fifth Earl was killed by an elk. There was no money in the bank, and Hogg Hall was slowly crumbing into ruins. The cost of running the house was around £3 million per year. The fact that the Sixth Earl had managed to keep the house from falling down ever since was something of a miracle. He did it using a combination of determination, cunning and wit. But mostly, he kept the lawyers and debtors at bay by means of lying, cheating, embezzlement and fraud.

Hardy even managed to add to Hogg Hall in 2008 by building a formal flower garden around the West Wing and a small, domed observatory on the south-east bank of the lake. Being a child of the space race in the sixties, the Sixth Earl knew quite a lot about astronomy. He would retire to the observatory for days on end, making snacks with a Breville Deep Fill Sandwich Toaster, looking at the stars through his reflecting telescope and occasionally watching hardcore pornography on his MacBook.

But back to the fishing trip. By now, there was a large pile of dead trout by the side of the lake.

"We need to make a fire and cook this lot," slurred Ingleby-Barwick.

"I'm all over it," said Melton, and he reached into the shopping trolley.

"What's that?" asked Hogg-Marchmont.

"Petrol," replied Thornaby, waving a big metal can. He poured a generous amount of the fuel over the fish and casually threw on a match. The resulting explosion blew all three men about nine feet away from the fire, setting Hogg-Marchmont's hair alight and neatly removing the eyebrows of Lord and Lady Ingleby-Barwick. Thornaby appeared unharmed, but as he wandered back towards the shopping trolley, it was clear that his bottom was on fire. The heady smell of cooking fish and gasoline filled the air.

"Trout for dinner!" enthused Hogg-Marchmont, pouring a glass of Hungarian Malbec over his head to put out the flames.

An hour later, the party began to sag rather. The fish supper had been disappointing to say the least, and Melton's style of al fresco cooking had received mixed reviews from the others.

Ingleby-Barwick had twice nearly choked on a fish bone, and when Hogg-Marchmont performed the Heimlich manoeuvre on him, he broke several of his friend's ribs.

"Is it just me," whispered Melton, "or has Hogg-Marchmont got a great big raging stiffy in his pants?"

"I thought I was imagining it," heaved Ingleby-Barwick, wincing from the pain in his side, "I didn't like to say anything."

The pair were not imagining it. Unwisely thinking that his wife would be uncontrollably delighted to see him when he returned from the dead, Hogg-Marchmont had taken two Viagra tablets before entering the library that morning. The resulting erection had since stubbornly refused to subside, and even after half a dozen bottles of wine, the Sixth Earl was still walking around like a tripod. As the trio sat on the grass to recover from the traumas of dinner, Hogg-Marchmont, in sheer desperation, suddenly began punching his penis.

"Get down, you bastard!" he cried. "Your presence is not required at this moment in time."

Ingleby-Barwick watched in silence for a while and then he offered a suggestion. "Why don't you hit it with a cricket bat?" he said.

"That's not a bad idea," agreed Melton, "put the poor thing out of its misery."

"I've had this erection since 9am this morning," slurred Hogg-Marchmont. "It reminds me of sitting on the school bus and having to hide my hard-on under a satchel."

"Ah, we've all trodden that path," daydreamed Melton, skilfully snorting a line of cocaine from the back of his hand, and then sneezing the whole lot into a bush. When he was that age, Melton had owned a special lunch tin with a circular hole in the bottom. While he was on the bus, he would put his erection through the hole, and if he became too aroused, he would raise the lid of the tin, slip his hand inside and quietly pay homage to himself.

"I didn't get an erection until I was thirty," confessed Ingleby-Barwick. "I thought it was a tumour."

Melton took the situation by the scruff of the neck. "So, do you want us to hit your joystick with cricket bats, or not?"

It was almost dark now, and Hogg-Marchmont had had a very long and problematic day. He'd returned from the dead, been attacked by his wife, and he'd just spent a full innings beating trout. He felt tired, drunk and defeated, and he had a tent pole in his trousers the size of Moby Dick.

"Hell," he said, "it just might work. What harm can it do?"

Melton and Ingleby-Barwick stood either side of Hogg-Marchmont.

"Are you going to take it out of your trousers?" asked the African. Melton looked a little green around the gills.

"Is that really necessary?" asked Hardy. "Can't you see where it is?"

"Oh, we can see it," giggled Ingleby-Barwick, "I just think this exercise might be more effective if you were to unleash it."

Straight from the bottle, Hogg-Marchmont took a healthy slug of Koonunga Hill Shiraz, and then he whipped out the offending member. As soon as he set eyes upon it, Melton Thornaby was sick. Then there was a blinding flash as Ingleby-Barwick took a photograph. The Sixth Earl leapt to his feet, fell over and then leapt to his feet again.

A full moon was beginning to rise over the lake, and in a profound, primal expression of frustration, anger and desperation, Hogg-Marchmont howled at it. Then he looked down and realised that his erection was gone. Before the Sixth Earl had time to howl at the moon again, there was a massive crash, followed by the sound of falling masonry and breaking glass. The three men slowly turned around to look at Hogg Hall, which was brightly illuminated in the moonlight.

"Where's the East Wing?" asked Melton Thornaby.

"Oh, bollocks!" said Hogg-Marchmont.

Chapter Three

The collapse of the East Wing was far from convenient. For a start, it made the whole house look asymmetrical, the West Wing now seeming awkward and self-conscious.

Reasons for the collapse were unclear. That part of the building was so unstable, that it could have been brought about by a sparrow landing on the roof, or a rodent taking a small bite out of one of the skirting boards.

Ironically, the only structure left standing after the collapse was the scaffolding that had recently been put up in order to effect cosmetic repairs. When the builders arrived on site for the first time the following morning, they at first panicked, thinking that they were going to be expected to rebuild the entire East Wing. It was quickly explained to them that all they needed to do was collect up all the bricks and tiles and put them into a great big pile in the middle of the garden.

Luckily, none of the Hogg-Marchmont family lived in the East Wing. It was mostly inhabited by about two hundred of Lady Celestia May's cats. These creatures have a very finely honed sixth sense, and all two hundred of them vacated the premises mere moments before the structure clattered to the ground.

The East Wing had an auspicious history. It was built by the Second Earl, who loved to entertain, and in 1830, he added ninety-seven luxurious guest bedrooms to the eastern extent of the house. People invited to stay at Hogg Hall spent their days hunting, fishing, riding horses, but mostly drinking. Legend tells that none of them were ever allowed to leave until they had downed a yard of ale, and the Second Earl had soundly bummed them on the billiard table in the Great Snooker Room.

In the evening, formal dinners would take place, followed by music and charades. The guests would then gather in the library to look at the Earl's world-famous Great Bohemian Chandelier.

There being no television in those days, large groups of people would often stand around and simply stare at chandeliers. This particular magnificent example was gifted to the Second Earl by Prince Agra of Tandoor, and was a birthday cake-shaped crystal fixture, which had once illuminated the Royal Poobah Palace in Istanbul.

"It comprises 750 crystal candleholders," the Second Earl would proudly tell his guests, and they would stand around for hours looking at it, while the servants offered them finger snacks and fine wines. One female guest had once been so transfixed by the ornament that she'd gone into a trance and had to be revived by means of smelling salts and brandy. On another occasion, the Belgian ambassador unwittingly ejaculated from sheer excitement, after first setting eyes upon the piece. After a couple of hours looking at the chandelier, the women would go to bed, and the men would gather in the library to smoke hundreds of cigars. It was quite common for guests to die of nicotine poisoning or asphyxiation during these sessions, and in the grounds, one could still see the remains of a small garden called 'The Smoker's Cemetery'. The walls and ceiling of the library are to this day still coated with a thick, mustard-coloured layer of nicotine.

In the late nineteenth century, social change and taxes began to affect the Hogg-Marchmont's lavish lifestyle. When the Second Earl died, over £1 million in death duties became due. Nonetheless, life continued much as before. The staff at Hogg Hall at this time consisted of three butlers, three under butlers, four valets, five footmen, twelve housekeepers, seventy-three housemaids, nine sewing women, eleven cooks, six kitchen maids, three vegetable maids, twenty-four scullery maids, six dairy maids, thirteen laundry maids and the Earl's private secretary Doris.

All of these people lived in the house with the gout-ridden Third Earl and his family, but other staff would also come in during the day, including twelve grooms, four chauffeurs, eight gamekeepers, six upholsterers, thirty-one scrubbing women, two laundry porters, three steam boiler men, a hundred and six window cleaners and a team of joiners, plumbers and electricians. In 1896, the number of gardeners peaked at fifteen hundred.

*

The Sixth Earl had a bastard of a hangover. He also had a very sore pecker, but for the life of him, he couldn't remember why. He awoke on the Great Sofa in the Great Lounge – a particularly uncomfortable piece of furniture with hard wooden armrests and very little padding. What was it with the Victorians and sofas?

The Great Lounge was where Celestia May kept her beloved houseplants. Feeling that it was little more than common assault to prune them, the plants had become so monstrously overgrown that it was now quite hard to move around the room without tripping over a frond or banging one's head on an overhanging branch. There were ferns; there were palms; there were grasses; and there was bamboo. Crawling menacingly across the mantelpiece was a giant trailing philodendron, and the sideboard was almost entirely engulfed in Swedish ivy.

Celestia May had once had a birthday party in the Great Lounge, and one of her friends had become lost. She finally emerged from the undergrowth two days later, her arms speared with a myriad of cactus spines, her eyes blinking painfully in the sunlight.

Just to double-check that the previous night's disaster was not simply some alcohol-fuelled fantasy, Hardy dragged himself from the Great Sofa, and after doing battle with a Chinese evergreen and two Madagascar dragon trees, he walked along the long, portrait-lined East Corridor.

A painting of the First Earl frowned down on him as he approached the door at the far end. Taking a deep breath, he threw it open. Sure enough, the East Wing was now nothing more than a pile of bricks and tiles, surrounded by stout perimeter scaffolding.

The East Wing gone, it was now possible to see the sea from that part of the house, and Hardy stood for a while and enjoyed an uninterrupted view of the spectacular rock that balanced precariously on top of Muddleton Point. The rock had been delicately balanced there for millions of years until it was dislodged one night in 1824 by the Second Earl and a group of his mischievous companions. However, following complaints from the residents of Muddleton, for whom the rock had become a tourist attraction and source of income, the Second Earl was forced, at great expense, to restore it.

"I want a divorce," said Countess Isabella.

"I didn't do this," explained Hardy, indicating the smoking ruins of the East Wing. "I wasn't anywhere near it. We were down at the lake. A fishing trip."

Hardy gently closed the doors so that he wouldn't have to think about the East Wing anymore.

"Melton Thornaby is being treated for third-degree burns," said Isabella, "Ingleby-Barwick is in casualty with three broken ribs. Gunshots were reported near the lake last night. And when I say 'lake', it seems that the entire ornamental lake has once again disappeared. And you call that a fishing trip?"

"What else would you call it?" asked Hogg-Marchmont.

Isabella folded her arms. "Oh, and while we're on the subject of the lake, just whose ashes did I sprinkle down there on Friday morning?"

"Don't leave me. I need you!" said Hardy, and then he thought hard for a moment. "Are you having an affair?" he asked.

Countess Isabella began to laugh. She laughed and she

laughed until she could laugh no longer, and a little bit of pee came out. Then she started to cry. She cried and she cried until she could cry no longer, and a little bit more pee came out. When Isabella finally stopped crying, she opened her eyes and Hardy had gone. He hated a scene. The Sixth Earl had jumped into the dented Daimler and had set off to see his mistress.

When Hardy arrived at Box-Girder Abbey, Lady Prunella was trying on hats. She liked to try on hats every day and had been doing so from a very early age.

"Oh, Prunella!" said Hogg-Marchmont.

"I'm trying on hats," replied his mistress.

"Isabella wants a divorce!" he cried, and he reached out his arms for an embrace. Lady Box-Girder glared at the Sixth Earl. "I'm trying on hats," she repeated.

"I think my wife might be having an affair," said Hardy.

"Hats," said Prunella, and she pointed towards the French windows.

Hardy went outside and leaned against the weathered, stone balustrade of the balcony, which overlooked the formal grounds of Box-Girder Abbey. The gardens had been recently attended to, and the tall, conical-shaped hedges stood proud and fiercely sharp-edged. Hardy loved topiary. There was nothing quite as sensual as a well-manicured shrubbery. The trees, also, were keenly honed and the bushes razor-sharp.

Hardy lit a cigarette. In the dressing room behind him, Lady Prunella continued to try on hats for another twenty minutes, and then she wafted out onto the balcony.

"I suppose you want to go to the Blue Bedroom?" she said.

"That would be comforting," replied Hogg-Marchmont.

Sexual encounters between Lady Box-Girder and the Sixth Earl were well rehearsed and tightly choreographed. Since Prunella could tolerate no physical contact whatsoever, Hardy was simply allowed to watch her hitch up her skirt and display her underwear while he stood exactly eight feet away and quietly masturbated into a laundered napkin. There were two distinct flavours of this onerous ritual. Having hitched up her clothing, if Lady Box-Girder was feeling frisky she would quickly pull down the top of her pants, giving Hardy a momentary glimpse of her thicket. If she wasn't really in the mood, as was usually the case, Prunella would simply stand very still, her skirt bunched up around her waist, her pants on display, until Hardy had gratefully emptied his seed. On one occasion, in 1998, Lady Box-Girder agreed to this procedure after drinking a full schooner of Harvey's Bristol Cream. Her inhibitions unleashed, she lowered her underwear all the way to the floor, allowing Hogg-Marchmont an entirely uninterrupted panorama of Prunella's pudenda. Having overenthusiastically encroached to a distance of just five feet, the Sixth Earl ejaculated with such intensity that a tiny globule of sperm landed on Lady Box-Girder's kneecap, causing her to recoil so violently that she tripped over her own undergarments and cracked a bone in her elbow. The pair did not meet again for six months. The next time they went into the Blue Bedroom, Lady Prunella had taken the precaution of painting a white line on the floorboards, behind which Hardy would be compelled to stand during congress.

Lady Box-Girder's intense dislike of physical contact stemmed from an experience she'd had with her geography teacher while boarding at Roebuck School during the early 1980s.

Roebuck was set in a delightful location on the cliffs overlooking the English Channel to the west of Cyrille Regis. It was an extremely expensive private college for ladies, and Prunella loved it there. The girls played vigorously, both on the hockey field and with one another after lights out, and there were many and varied opportunities for the students to expand both their minds and their blossoming genitalia.

The blue sea twinkling outside, the geography room prided itself on having one of the best views of any school in the country, and it was here, every Thursday afternoon, that Prunella and the geography teacher Mr. Winchester would wedge a chair against the door, and on two desks, pushed hastily together and covered with a duvet, they would exchange the fluids of desire.

How they loved each other. Prunella was seventeen; Mr. Winchester was seventy-three. The affair went on for six months, and then Prunella discovered that she was pregnant with twins. Mr. Winchester refused to marry her, preferring instead to stay loyal to his sixty-three-year-old wife who was blind, in a wheelchair and also happened to be the headmistress of Roebuck School.

Prunella was heartbroken. She ran away from Roebuck, and Mr. Winchester used his Diner's Club Card to check her into a remote clinic on Bodmin Moor. Three weeks later, after brief but passionate affairs with both the caretaker at the clinic and the doctor who performed the abortion, Prunella returned to her parents at Box-Girder Abbey, vowing to never again allow herself to be touched by a man.

Mr. Winchester died of a stroke soon afterwards. He was found naked under a duvet on top of two desks pushed together in the geography room.

*

After visiting his mistress, Hardy Hogg-Marchmont went to Muddleton Cottage Hospital to visit Lord and Lady Ingleby-Barwick. Hardy found Angus in a small room adjacent to one of the wards. There was a very expensive-looking machine on a trolley next to his bed. A little screen showed that Ingleby-Barwick had no heartbeat, no brain activity and that his body temperature was zero degrees. An alarm was going off to warn the doctors.

Ingleby-Barwick sat up with a start when he heard Hardy come into the room.

"This machine says you're dead," observed the Sixth Earl.

"Oh, it's been making that bleeping noise ever since I was brought in here," Angus told his friend. "I think it's still registering readings from the chap who was in this bed before me."

"Should we tell someone?" asked Hardy.

"I tell them every time they come in," said Ingleby-Barwick. "One of the nurses tried to switch it off, but it gave her an electric shock."

"I brought you some soup," said Hardy, and he handed the patient a Thermos flask filled with Best Cream of

Broccoli. Most people take grapes to hospital, but Hardy knew that his friend's greatest passion in life was soup. But not just any soup. Ingleby-Barwick was an obsessive compulsive and proud of it. As such, he only ate soup that began with the letter B.

Bacon Soup, Beef Noodle, Bergan Fish, Bird's Nest, Borscht, Bouillabaisse and Brown Windsor, Angus adored them all.

"Isabella's leaving me," said Hardy, "she wants a divorce."

"Never going to happen," said Ingleby-Barwick. "The worse you behave, the more Isabella will love you. She'll be there for the duration. She'll stand by her man. She is your rock, your safe anchor in an almost perfect storm."

Hardy's phone went bleep and a text message flashed onto the screen.

"She's moved out," said Hardy. Then another message popped into the phone. *Lady Labia has gone into labour*, it said.

A stocky, tattooed male nurse came into the room. He put a thermometer under Hogg-Marchmont's tongue and took his pulse.

"I'm not the patient," said Hardy.

"Oh," said the nurse, a little surprised. "Who is the patient?"

"The African gentleman," said Hardy.

The nurse took the instrument out of Hardy's mouth, dried it on his uniform and shoved it into Angus's mouth.

"You should have gone private," said Hardy.

"This is private," shrugged Angus. The nurse wiped his nose on his sleeve and scratched his balls. "You have very small ears," he said to Hogg-Marchmont, and then he left.

"I am about to become a grandfather," announced Hardy.

Ingleby-Barwick jumped out of bed. "Right, that's it, I'm out of here," he said. "Let's go and celebrate."

*

Lady Labia stood legs astride, her body bent forward over the four-poster in Hatcher's bedroom at Hogg Hall. Two midwives knelt on their hands and knees behind her and peered into her chasm like two seasoned potholers planning their descent into the Gaping Chamber at Muddleton Gorge.

"Are you sure you wouldn't like to get onto the bed?" asked Tiffany, the younger of the two midwives.

"Don't touch me, bitch!" screamed Lady Labia.

When her waters had broken, in the middle of the food hall at Selfridges, Hatcher had decided on the spot that his wife should have the child at home. The pair had driven, at a breakneck pace, back to Hogg Hall, speed cameras flashing them every three or four miles, Labia screaming like a hungry seagull.

It was Lady Labia's first baby. She was not a dainty woman, and the doctor had assured her that she was 'broad enough in the beam for the baby to pop its little head out any time it liked'.

Indeed, the locals in the Pig & Pencil Case had been able to play 'Fat or Pregnant' for many weeks, prior to the good news being shared in the *Muddleton Gazette*.

Lady Labia was now in full labour, her cervix dilated to seven centimetres.

"Stop measuring my cervix!" she screamed at Tiffany. "And get this fucking thing out of me!"

"Don't push," said Blodwyn, the older midwife, with a soft and reassuring Welsh accent.

"If I want to push, I will fucking well push!" yelled Labia, and she dug her nails deep into Viscount Hatcher's hand, causing him to yelp, and for blood to gently trickle down to his wrist.

"You're doing great," said Hatcher.

"Fuck off and die," said Lady Labia.

"I can see the head!" shouted Tiffany.

"No, you can't," replied Blodwyn.

"Well, what's that, then?" asked Tiffany.

"Oh, yes, sorry that is the head," said Blodwyn. "I'll go and get the right specs from my bag."

Still in a fully standing position, her legs akimbo, her upper body bent forward over the side of the bed, Lady Labia began to scream. This was a deafening, high-pitched, extended, scream. A primal scream. The scream of a fatally injured pterodactyl.

"Uh, oh," said Tiffany. There was a faint tearing noise and, using nothing more than the power of gravity, the newest heir to Hogg Hall left Lady Labia's womb and hurtled head first towards the Victorian tiles on the floor of the bedroom.

Tiffany froze. It was her first delivery. Luckily Blodwyn had delivered over seven thousand babies and was by now on her way back to Lady Labia's side, wearing the correct glasses. She was, however, still at least five paces away when she saw the child exit Labia's vagina and begin its short journey towards the floor. Her hands outstretched before her, the midwife launched herself forward like a scrum half playing at Twickenham. Time stood still, as the infant appeared to hover and rotate between floor and fanny. In a triumphant display of perfect timing, Blodwyn's hands cupped the baby's head and caught it safely, not more than a nanosecond before it smashed onto the floor. There was silence for a few seconds, and then the infant gulped its lungs full of air and began to cry. Tiffany felt a little bit of sick rise up into her throat as she surveyed the damage to Lady Labia's curtains.

"You might need a few stitches there," she said.

Blodwyn clambered to her feet, holding onto the baby for dear life. "Would you like to cut the cord?" she asked Viscount Hatcher, and in the time-honoured fashion he fainted, cracking his head on the floor and knocking himself cold.

*

It was early evening at Hogg Hall. A time for long shadows, quiet contemplation and gin and tonic. Soft, Titian light illuminated the yellow sandstone on the west facade, and it glinted on the little pointy gothic towers on the roof. An hour earlier, a text had arrived on Hogg-Marchmont's phone which read simply, *It's a boy*.

There was also an auspicious birth that day in the beehive. It was the birth of a bee called Anthogrid. This tiny bee hatched from his egg at exactly 5.04pm, and he sniffed at the air suspiciously. Three days earlier, the queen had laid about two thousand other eggs too, and now almost every one of them was hatching. In his short life, it was unlikely that Anthogrid would learn the name of his father, the names of any of his two thousand brothers and sisters, or that he would ever find out that he lived in a beehive under a servant's bed in Hogg Hall.

Anthogrid tried to fly but nothing happened. "When will it be time for my wings?" he asked.

He could have been born as a dolphin, a lioness or a huge strutting stag with magnificent antlers. He could have been born as a goldfish or as a chartered surveyor. But Anthogrid was a humble bumble bee, and he was going to have to get used to it.

*

Thornaby, Ingleby-Barwick and the Sixth Earl sat in the library, the stained glass throwing red, blue and green light across the extendable mahogany table. The gin and tonic course duly completed, four empty bottles of celebratory Bollinger now sat on the floor, the air heavy with Cuban cigar smoke.

Above the fireplace a dark, imposing portrait of the Second Earl looked down on them. It was an artwork that told a lot about the Hogg-Marchmont dynasty. The Third Earl had carefully drawn a moustache onto the Second Earl's face, and there was also a cock and balls, scribbled by the Fourth Earl. The Fifth Earl had made no adornments, but Hardy Hogg-Marchmont, at the age of thirteen, had written the word 'tits' in Biro under the artist's signature in the bottom right-hand corner. Art experts had suggested many times that the portrait should be properly restored, but the family insisted that the graffiti of their ancestors was an integral part of the work's provenance.

The Great Mirror, which ran along almost the entire length of the Great South Wall, was fashioned from fine glass imported by the First Earl from Mesopotamia. It was made from lead oxide, potash and silica. No one had any idea what silica or potash was, but the Great Mirror looked spectacular all the same.

Being French, Lady Labia had a great appreciation of such splendour, and when she was in the room, she spent almost all the time admiring her reflection. When a team of restorers worked on the mirror in 2014, one of them suggested that Lady Labia was in serious danger of wearing the mirror out, and for the purposes of preservation, they suggested covering it up from time to time.

Thousands of ancient, dust-covered books lined the walls of the Great Library, none of which had ever been read by a single member of the Hogg-Marchmont family. The Third Earl had once tried to read a fine old leather-bound edition of *The Oresteia* but he soon lost concentration and resorted instead to smoking opium. Earl Hardy had once attempted to reach *Pears' Cyclopaedia* on the top shelf but had fallen off the little rosewood ladder and knocked himself out on a French porcelain mantel clock.

The Great Library was a vast, aircraft hangar of a room, and it always felt a little empty. Even when it was full of guests, it still echoed like a cathedral. But now that Countess Isabella was gone, the room felt more empty than ever. Celestia May had left with her mother. Hardy didn't know where they'd gone, but he guessed they'd be spending some time at Isabella's cousin's villa in Spain.

Hatcher was out celebrating fatherhood with a group of his noisiest and most loathsome friends – his exhausted wife left alone upstairs to recuperate, the baby attended to by a well-groomed, middle-aged nanny called Alice, to whom Hardy had been introduced earlier, and with whom he had every intention of copulating.

"Don't you want to go upstairs and see the baby?" asked Ingleby-Barwick.

"I don't like babies," said Hardy.

"Would sir like me to open another bottle of the Bollinger?" enquired O'Donnell.

"How many bottles are left?" asked Hogg-Marchmont.

"There are eight more," said O'Donnell, as precise as ever.

"Just keep 'em coming," said Thornaby.

"Very well," said O'Donnell, and he turned to go out of the room.

"Oh, I meant to give you this, sir," he said, and he handed a large brown envelope to his master. "It was delivered by hand this afternoon."

Hogg-Marchmont was always very suspicious of brown envelopes. They rarely delivered good news. He reluctantly tore open the envelope and read the papers inside, of which there seemed to be many. The others watched him with interest while O'Donnell popped open another bottle and filled both their glasses with more fizz.

"Parking fine?" asked Angus.

"No," smiled Hardy, "it's from the council. Hogg Hall has been deemed an unsafe structure. It's been condemned to be demolished."

Everyone looked at everyone else.

"What utter rubbish," boomed Melton Thornaby, thumping the table. A small piece of plaster fell from the ceiling and landed in his drink.

The door opened and Nanny Alice came in, holding a tiny bundle.

"I thought you'd like to meet your grandson," she said, and she gently parted the blanket. The baby's cheeks were covered in reassuringly bushy hair.

"At least that proves he's a Hogg-Marchmont," said Hardy.

The baby vomited, filled its nappy and began to cry. It cried like only a newborn can cry – a repetitive, insistent, invasive shrieking that eats its way into your brain and makes you want to burst into tears and rip your own head off.

"What's it called?" asked Hardy.

Nurse Alice comforted the infant by putting her pinkie into his mouth. "Viscount Hatcher has named him Keith," she said.

"He looks like Simon Pegg," said the Sixth Earl, and the others gathered around to see.

"Bugger me, he does look like Simon Pegg," agreed Thornaby and Ingleby-Barwick.

"All newborn babies look like Simon Pegg," said the nurse, and she grinned at Hardy in a way that made his trousers twitch and momentarily allowed him to forget that his first grandson had been born just in time to see the ancestral home torn down by a council bulldozer.

Hardy suddenly felt that he needed some fresh air. "Would you excuse me," he said, and he strode out of the room.

Ten minutes later, he sat alone in the Tithe Barn, a conspicuous landmark in the grounds of Hogg Hall which was very useful for storing tithes. The Sixth Earl looked up at the ancient curved timbers in the roof, and he tried to visualise what it would be like to watch his house being demolished. He'd let down his wife; he'd let down his son; but worst of all, he'd let down his ancestors.

A white barn owl flashed silently past and deftly plucked a field mouse from the ground. She carried it up into the rafters and perched on one of the transverse beams immediately above Hardy's head. The owl teased the tiny creature with its claws for a while before ripping out its entrails with its beak.

At least that mouse is having a worse day than I am, thought Hardy, his eyes slowly filling with tears. Then the owl shat on his head.

Chapter Four

"You cannot christen a member of the English nobility Keith!" said the Sixth Earl. In desperation, Hogg-Marchmont had telephoned his son, as Hatcher and Lady Labia Antoinette were driving into town to register the birth of their new arrival. Hardy's voice boomed out through the hands-free speakers in Hatcher's Jaguar XJR Saloon. "What does 'Keith' even mean?" he asked.

"It's a very proud and meaningful name," Hatcher told his father.

"But your wife can't even say the word Keith," said Hardy.

"Yes I can," replied Lady Labia. "Keeeesss."

The turbo kicked in on the Jag, and Hatcher overtook a tractor, narrowly missing a fast oncoming Audi. Lady Labia screamed. The tightly bundled creature in the baby seat began to cry.

"Name me one notable person from history called Keith," asked Hardy.

"Keith Habersberger," replied Hatcher.

"Who's he?" screamed his father.

"Comedian," said Hatcher.

"Never heard of him," said Hardy.

Hatcher had taken the precaution of writing down a list of Keiths. As he peered down at it, he took his eyes off the road and the XJR narrowly missed an overtaking Lexus. Lady Labia howled again, and as Hatcher braked hard, the baby projectile vomited over the back of his mother's head.

"There's Keith Urban, Keith Dee, Keith Leak, Keith Sweat, Keith Duffy, Keith Powers, Keith Ape."

"Keith Ape?" said Hardy. "Surely that's a made-up name."

"No, these are actual names of famous people," said his son. "I looked it up. Keith Ape is a rap artist in South Korea."

Hardy had heard of Keith Dee. He presented the breakfast show on Muddleton FM, which was particularly challenging because he suffered from Tourette's syndrome. Hardy enjoyed the show very much, and often telephoned the studio hoping that Keith would give him a shout-out.

Hatcher had just two further cards to play. "Keith Moon," he offered.

"Total nut job," insisted Hardy.

"Alright, Keith Chegwin," said Hatcher.

"You're shitting me," said the Sixth Earl. "Why would you want to name your son and heir after Keith Chegwin?"

"It is up to us what we name our son," snapped Lady Labia. "I will not be dictated to by a man with tiny ears."

The Sixth Earl pleaded with his son, "Well at least come up with a longer version of the name so you can shorten it to Keith," he suggested. "What about Keithland or Keithmont? Or maybe Keithman or Keithford or Keithington?"

"It's just going to be Keith," said Hatcher. "It's decided. I've already bought the name."

"What do you mean, you've bought it?" puzzled Hardy.

Hatcher had googled 'Keith' and had stumbled upon a web page with the title 'Make sure you get the right name for your baby'.

The name Keith, it explained, *is aggressive and independent. It's a name for big men with big ambitions, large-scale ideas and excellent business judgment. This name will enable you to gain the financial accumulation to which you feel entitled.*

At the bottom of the page there was a big green button labelled 'Buy This Name'. Hatcher clicked on it and was taken to a PayPal portal which offered to safely and securely sell him the name 'Keith'. As his finger hovered over the 'Buy' button, Lady Labia happened to glance at the screen of Hatcher's iPad.

"What are you doing?" she asked.

"I thought we'd decided that we were going to name the baby Keith," he said.

"We are," replied Lady Labia.

"Well, I'm buying the name," Hatcher explained.

"How much is it?" asked Labia.

"£11.99," replied Hatcher. "Plus VAT."

The Sixth Earl sighed. "Hatcher, you do not need to purchase baby names. They're free."

His son laughed. "Father, I really think you should leave complicated things like the internet to me."

There was very little point arguing with Hatcher. Growing up at Hogg Hall, he had so little experience of the real world that giving him any kind of information at all simply confused him. Hatcher's car was now on the duel carriageway just outside Muddleton-on-the-Marsh. He was in the fast lane, trying to overtake an old Fiat 850, and he was tailgating the tiny vehicle in the most frightening and intimidating way possible – headlights flashing, the XJR just inches away from the Fiat's rear bumper. You can tell a lot about a man from the way he drives and this, ladies and gentlemen, was the cretin that was Viscount Hatcher Hogg-Marchmont.

"Look at that cretin behind us in the Jag," said the bald man in the Fiat.

"Oh, just pull over, Geoffrey," said the man's elderly mother, but Geoffrey did not like to be bullied. He moved as if to pull over but then stayed exactly where he was and reduced speed. Hatcher pulled into the slow lane to try and overtake on the inside, but the Fiat flashed its left indicator and touched its break lights twice.

Then the car moved slowly across to the inside lane in front of Hatcher's Jag. Infuriated, the Viscount quickly accelerated and shot past the Fiat, catching the car's driver side rear bumper as he did so and sending the vehicle spinning off the road and into a cornfield.

Neither Viscount Hatcher nor Lady Labia noticed what had happened to the Fiat. It was quite simply outside of their arena of interest. They also didn't know who the prime minister of Great Britain was.

Half an hour later, the noble couple sat in front of Mr. A.G. Crow, Registrar of Births, Deaths and Marriages at

Muddleton Old Town Hall. Their new arrival sat gurgling quietly in its baby seat.

"You'd think it would be chronological," remarked Hatcher.

"I'm sorry?" asked the registrar.

"You'd think they'd list them in the order they happen," he explained. "Why is it the Registrar of Births, Deaths and Marriages, and not the Registrar of Births, Marriages and Deaths?"

"I have a head cold," said the registrar, "do you mind if we get on?"

Mr. Crow opened a brown folder full of birth certificates and tapped his Biro onto his tongue to moisten it. Hatcher had only ever seen people do that in 1950's comedies starring Leslie Phillips.

"Name of father?" enquired the registrar.

"Hatcher Bosch Hardy Mills Hogg-Marchmont," he said proudly.

"Mister?" asked the registrar.

"Viscount," corrected Hatcher.

"Nationality?" asked Crow.

"English," stated Hatcher.

There was a short pause. "I'll put down British," said the registrar. "Occupation?"

Hatcher thought for a moment. "Aristocrat," he said, and he peered out of the window like Lord Nelson on the bridge of *HMS Victory*. The registrar sniffed and wrote down 'Unemployed'.

He tapped the pen onto his tongue again. "Name of mother?" he enquired.

Lady Labia felt awkward in the presence of British

officialdom. It made her feel like an illegal immigrant. She spoke her full name nervously, "Lady Labia Antoinette Dominique Lyonnais Fabienne Josephine Pissoir de Fondu."

"Nationality?" asked Crow.

"Seriously?" said Hatcher, and the registrar wrote down 'French'.

"Occupation?" asked the registrar.

"Author," replied Lady Labia, and Hatcher squeezed her hand proudly.

After completing her history degree in Marseille, Labia had written a book about the sex life of French playwright Molière. Actually, she had started a book on Moliere but had grown bored with it after nine pages, and her father, Marquis Antoine Pissoir de Fondu, had hired a ghost writer to complete the book for her. Since the ghost writer was a world-famous French biographer, it's not surprising that the book reached number one in the bestseller list. Lady Labia followed up her literary success by starting, and not finishing, books on Jules Verne, Louis XIV and Charles de Gaulle, all of which were critically acclaimed and propelled her to fame in her native France. But when her father the Marquis lost all his money in an infamous property scam in the Vendee, Labia Antoinette decided to leave France forever. She met Viscount Hatcher three years later at an Elvis Costello gig at the Royal Albert Hall. During 'Watching the Detectives', her long hair somehow become entangled in the gold strap of Hatcher's oversized Rolex, and the pair were manacled together throughout the evening, finally managing to pull apart from one another during the closing chords of 'Oliver's Army'.

It would be wrong to say that Hatcher and Labia Antoinette were deeply in love. Lady Labia liked to fuck, and Hatcher was fiercely supportive of her in this pursuit. But they did, surprisingly, have quite a lot in common, which made them a half-decent match. They'd both been spoiled by their parents; they were both terminally lazy; and, to be frank, they were both as stupid as spoons.

Hatcher left Trinity College just three weeks into his first year, genuinely believing that he'd completed his course. What had given him the idea that you could study law in three weeks was a mystery, but to this day, he still went around telling everyone that he had a degree from Cambridge.

Hatcher didn't really have a firm grasp of what money was. If he wanted a new car, he would simply key a PIN number into a card reader and his nice new vehicle would appear in the drive. In fact, remembering the four digits of his PIN number was probably the most challenging thing that Viscount Hatcher ever had to do in his life. He had still not yet worked out that his father's failed faking of his own death, and the imminent demise of Hogg Hall, had anything whatsoever to do with the seemingly bottomless bank account from which he and his wife paid their bills. In Hatcher's mind, the two things were entirely unconnected. He'd never once checked the balance of his bank account and he had no intention of ever doing so.

"And the name of the baby?" asked the registrar of births.

"Keith," said Hatcher, and he proudly held up the receipt he'd printed off for £11.99 + VAT. The registrar took the document from him, folded it neatly, and with a smile, he put it into a drawer in his desk. The baby began to cry again. He did not know it yet, but he might be the first Hogg-Marchmont in history never to inherit Hogg Hall.

The Sixth Earl chose to ignore the text message on his phone. He had a nasty feeling that it would be telling him the name on his grandson's new birth certificate, and he really did not want to see it. More importantly, there was work to be done. Hardy had to go and judge the vegetables.

*

Since the nineteenth century, the fruit and veg at the Muddleton Agricultural Show had been judged by a Hogg-Marchmont, and the fact that the Sixth Earl had recently died in a riding accident was not going to stop him from attending the show. The Fourth Earl had been a keen vegetable grower, and his opinion on carrots, marrows and turnips was beyond reproach. Hardy, on the other hand, did not like vegetables; he knew very little about vegetables; and he did not trust vegetables. This was probably because his mother had forced him to eat vegetables and his son had the IQ of a cauliflower.

Muddleton Agricultural Show was the town's largest annual event. People didn't go to it because they wanted to look at cows and sheep, or because they enjoyed the sight of an eighty-year-old man on a motorbike riding through a hoop of fire. They went because nothing else happened in Muddleton. It had rained for the event every year since records began, except for 1963 when there was a blizzard. With the rain came the mud, and Muddleton had so much mud they could have seriously considered exporting it.

Some said that the town had actually been named after the mud, but there was no compelling evidence for this theory. The late Sixth Earl waded through the showground and surveyed the very best the town had to offer. Virtually everyone said good day to him. Sure enough, they'd already forgotten that he was dead.

The Muddleton Goat Society were out in strength, as were Mrs. Craddock's Flea-Ridden Basset Hounds and Sod Cotton's Distractingly Lame Shire Horses. One of Mr. Timms' Homing Pigeons was being eaten by one of Mr. Sutton's Performing Birds of Prey, and two twelve-year-old trainees from the St. John's Ambulance Brigade were attempting to revive an elderly trombone player from the Royal British Legion Marching Band.

O'Donnell had planned to exhibit his bees at the agricultural show, but he was worried that moving the hive to the common might disturb them. He was also scared that Countess Isabella would be furious if she ever discovered that he'd found a home for the inhabitants of the Great Hive.

*

Deep in the brood chamber, Anthogrid and his two thousand brothers and sisters were being fed by a swarm of stout nurse bees – a palatable cocktail of honey and bee milk which the nurses produced in food glands located in their heads. As he digested the mixture, he watched as the field bees returned from their sorties, their thighs sticky with nectar, and he dreamed of the day when he too would first soar from the hive and forage for pollen.

His feed completed, Anthogrid curled up and tried to go to sleep, but there were two bees arguing noisily in the next hexagonal cell. It was Arvid and Egil.

"That's nonsense," insisted Arvid, "Earth, Wind & Fire's 1973 release *Head to the Sky* was a far superior album."

"Yes, but it only got to number twenty-seven in the US charts," said Egil.

For some reason that no one fully understands, all bumble bees are born with an intimate knowledge of the work of Grammy-award-winning soul band Earth, Wind & Fire. This is one of nature's great miracles, but it can lead to some very heated discussions in the hive.

"OK, what's your favourite album?" asked Arvid.

"Easy," replied Egil, "*Boogie Wonderland: The Very Best of Earth Wind & Fire.*"

"That's a compilation album!" cried Arvid. "You can't count compilation albums!"

*

On his way to visit the larger of the two vegetable marquees, the late Earl Hardy Hogg-Marchmont stopped off at the beer tent where Melton Thornaby was holding court in his usual place at the bar, accompanied by Ingleby-Barwick, who was wearing a tall, powdered wig and full seventeenth-century costume. The trio each drank nine or ten pints of Raddles Chewy Dark Summer Ale, and Hardy brought them up to speed on his recent discussions re: the naming of his grandson.

"Keith?" hiccupped Melton. "Do you know, that's one of my all-time favourite names. Good show, old man."

Back in the day, Melton had been a good friend of a celebrity chef and renowned alcoholic called Keith Floyd, and the pair had shared many a scoop of claret together. At least someone liked the name.

Three hours later, his hands clasped behind his back like royalty, the late Sixth Earl strolled drunkenly along a row of almost identical cabbages.

"That one's the biggest," he announced grandly, and he pinned a rosette on it, as ever still not fully understanding that the first prize was supposed to be awarded for quality and not quantity. He stumbled onwards, arbitrarily awarding rosettes of various colours to pumpkins, tomatoes, cucumbers and Brussels sprouts.

"Right, that's it, job done," he whispered to the white-coated vegetables coordinator, and he spotted Melton and Angus standing at the entrance to the tent, holding up three steaming glass cups of what smelt like Mrs. Comerford's Hot Rum Punch.

"Wait," said the vegetables coordinator, "you haven't judged the cress."

"The cress?" roared Hogg-Marchmont. "Who gives a fuck about cress?"

What had previously been a very noisy and bustling tent fell silent. Councillor Prodding, Chairman of the Cress Society, and incidentally the elected Mayor of Muddleton, stood up from behind his stall and marched over to Hardy. Every eye in the room was upon him.

"Sir," he began, "you may not care anything about cress, but I can assure you that many people in this town do."

Hardy laughed long and hard, then he clambered precariously onto a chair. "Ladies and gentlemen," he proclaimed, "I have something to ask you all. Please raise your hand in the air if you give a flying fuck about cress."

There were about a hundred people in the vegetable tent. They all looked at each other, and nobody really knew what to do. This was, after all, the late Hardy Hogg-Marchmont, Sixth Earl of Hogg Hall. Were they supposed to raise their hands? What might be the consequences of their vote? Councillor Prodding raised his hand, and everyone looked at him. Then two others put their arms in the air, one of whom was a four-year-old boy.

"There you are, Prodding," slurred Hogg-Marchmont, "it appears that interest in cress is on the wane." Then he fell off the chair he was standing on and landed with a thump atop a display of radishes and sweet potatoes. An almost identical incident had taken place the previous year involving lettuce.

Melton and Ingleby-Barwick helped Hardy to his feet. The trio lit a couple of large Arturo Fuentes cigars, and they splashed their way through the puddles that surrounded the beer tent. The fire engines turned up surprisingly quickly. Four of them. By the time they arrived, sirens blaring, the beer tent was already fully ablaze – an event that was virtually inevitable from the first moment Hogg-Marchmont and his cronies had spotted the fireworks.

"I think they're probably for later," giggled Ingleby-Barwick.

"But it'll be dark later," whispered Hardy, "let's let them off now."

The Sixth Earl grabbed an armful of rockets, and never one to miss out on a good wheeze, Thornaby and Angus did the same.

"Shouldn't we let them off outside the tent?" suggested Melton.

"It's raining outside," reasoned Hogg-Marchmont, and he stuck a large rocket into the ground and lit it with his cigar. He was expecting it fly straight upwards, cutting a neat little hole in the canvas of the marquee as it went. Instead, the firework veered off at a forty-five-degree angle, ricocheted off the canvas and exploded on top of the wooden bar. One or two people laughed, but most of them screamed and ran for the exit. There were a few minor burns.

"My turn!" shouted Melton, and he launched three rockets at the same time. The first set a chair on fire; the second set a table ablaze; and the third blew Mrs. Tibbins' hat off.

"What the Hell are you doing?" shouted Councillor Bottomley.

"A firework display!" yelled Hogg-Marchmont delightedly, and he set off a dozen more rockets which whistled around inside the marquee like shooting stars in a pinball machine. A police siren could suddenly be heard approaching from the direction of the village.

"Time to scarper," chuckled Hogg-Marchmont, tapping his nose, and he and his three companions headed for cover behind a small spinney of trees on the far corner of the common.

*

"We cannot murder Father," Hatcher whispered to his wife as the pair sat up in bed that evening. Keith

Hogg-Marchmont was sucking furiously on his mother's breast, something that Hatcher himself would normally be doing at that time of night. He was already beginning to feel that he was being replaced by this cacophonous and unbeautiful little fellow.

"You cannot be found guilty of killing a dead man," said Lady Labia, "then you will be the Seventh Earl."

"Technically I am already the Seventh Earl," Hardy pointed out. "I have Father's death certificate to prove it. The problem is that, him being dead doesn't actually seem to count for anything around here. The locals just refer to him as the late Earl, and they still expect him to go and judge the marrows on the village green."

Lady Labia hissed like a Disney villain. "As long as that detestable man breathes, you will never be free to make anything of your life. With your father out of the way, you can sell the land, and we can go and live somewhere with white sands and palm trees."

"Bournemouth?" asked Hatcher.

"No!" screamed Labia, switching her son swiftly from left to right nipple. "We shall go to the Caribbean and live like kings."

*

Since both of their passports had expired, Lady Isabella and her daughter were not in Spain as Hardy had suspected. They were in fact sleeping not five hundred yards away in the Second Earl's Great Folly. The tower was now almost entirely derelict, and the once stylish and elegant Fisting Room had two seagulls living in it. But the Circular

Bedroom was at least still watertight, and Celestia May and her mother had chucked a couple of sleeping bags onto the big round bed. Celestia May slumped on the mattress and looked at herself in the cracked and stained circular mirror on the ceiling. Six flickering candles struggled to illuminate the room.

"Mother, when are we going home?" she asked the Countess.

"When I'm good and ready," replied her mother, and she placed a little kettle on the portable camp stove in the fireplace.

"What will happen next?" asked Celestia May.

"Oh, your father will probably be charged with fraud and get arrested as usual," replied Isabella.

"I had a text from Mary Prodding this afternoon," said Celestia.

"Do I know her?" asked the Countess.

"Her father is Mayor of Muddleton," explained her daughter. "She's in charge of measuring seaweed at the marine institute."

"Oh, yes, I remember," Isabella recalled. "Lovely girl, very thick ankles."

"Mary says she saw Father at the agricultural show today," revealed Celestia May.

"Did anyone else see him?" asked the Countess.

"Everyone did," her daughter replied. "Apparently, he climbed onto a chair and shouted at the top of his voice. Then he let off some fireworks and burnt down the vegetable tent. Mary says there were several people there who were actually at father's funeral, and no one batted an eyelid. They just talked about cress."

"Cress?" exclaimed the Countess.

"Cress," confirmed Celestia May.

The Countess put a piece of bread onto a toasting fork and held it close to the tiny flame on the camping stove. A pipistrelle bat fluttered into the room and attached itself to the distressed plaster cornice above the fireplace.

"That's the trouble with the peasants around here," sneered Isabella, "they still imagine that Hogg Hall holds some kind of power over them. If only they knew the sad truth."

*

Nelly Frapp generally got out of bed to go to the toilet about six times a night. As the Earl's cook and housekeeper approached her ninetieth year, her bladder had shrivelled to the size of a prawn. This situation was made worse if, at the end of the day, O'Donnell forgot to go outside into the front courtyard and switch off the fountain.

The Great Fountain was one of the most enchanting architectural features of Hogg Hall. At its centre were four Saddleback sows, carved from the finest marble. These creatures had once spewed impressive jets high into the air, but now, like the Sixth Earl, their output was little more than a disappointing drizzle. The fountain was home to a pair of rare Gressingham Ducks and an elderly mallard called Ned.

The nocturnal trickle of the Great Fountain did nothing to help Mrs. Frapp's incontinence, and she often wished that the Third Earl had never built the bloody thing in the first place. Mrs. Frapp had been a very fit and healthy woman in her day. She'd previously cooked for the Fifth Earl, and in her youth, she'd been able to dash around the below-stairs corridors of Hogg Hall like an Olympic sprinter on unsanctioned prescription medication. Nelly was seventeen when she first joined the staff as a kitchen maid. Her annual salary was £5, and she worked from 4.30am until 11.55pm with one afternoon off every three years. Nelly assumed many everyday duties such as preparing vegetables, plucking game and poultry and baking around sixty loaves of bread per day. She was also responsible for sweeping and cleaning the kitchen, the larder, the corridors, the roof, guttering, drains, sewers and for polishing the twenty-six huge marble steps that rose to the front entrance of the house. She had to scrub tables, shelves and cupboards, and she had to shoot any rodents that happened to wander into the kitchen. In her spare time, Nelly would also be expected to make cakes for luncheon, tea and dessert, rolls for breakfast, and knit scarves, gloves and socks for the family.

Nelly was only allowed upstairs once a week. This was for morning prayers and to be soundly spanked by the Fifth Earl. Otherwise, she spent all her time between the kitchen and the tiny bedroom in the attic, which she shared with eleven others. Nelly would get one square meal a week, which she would eat under the stairs with the scullery maid and the chimney sweep.

The Burlington grandfather clock in the Great Corridor showed 2.03am as Nelly slowly and deliberately made her way to the servants' lavatory on the first floor. Her Zimmer frame's *clunk, clunking* on the floorboards kept in strict 4/4 rhythm by the timepiece's loud, metronome-like ticking. As always, it took Nelly around twenty minutes to get from her bedroom to the toilet, and then precisely four seconds to empty her tiny bladder. On the way back to bed, she passed the bedroom of Hardy Hogg-Marchmont.

Following his performance at the agricultural show and subsequent escape from the police, Hardy had dropped in on Lord and Lady Ingleby-Barwick, and both he and Melton Thornaby had been conscientiously overentertained, both with booze and broth. Soup of the Day was Brown Veal. He had then somehow managed to drive the dented Daimler back to Hogg Hall, and he'd arrived home at around 1am. The pig gargoyles watched silently as the Sixth Earl weaved and wobbled his way to the front door. When Hardy was drunk, which was every night, he had an extraordinary knack of falling up the staircase. He had no idea how he achieved this, and he knew that it defied the laws of physics, but it was just as well that he could do it, or he would have spent every night of his life sleeping on the bottom stair.

Unusually, the door to Hogg-Marchmont's bedroom was half open, and Nelly could hear him snoring loudly inside. But as the old servant piloted her Zimmer steadily past the door, she felt sure that she saw someone moving around inside the room. Nelly was blind in one eye, and the other eye had a cataract, but her brain was still as sharp as an egg slicer. She popped her head around the door. There was a small gap between the curtains, and a narrow beam of weak, sapphire moonlight illuminated the tapestry above the headboard. In the semi-darkness, Viscount Hatcher was standing next to his father's bed, a large feather pillow held out in front of him.

"You're up late, Master Hatcher," said Nelly from the doorway.

Hatcher vanished into the shadows, and the Sixth Earl grunted, growled and turned over in his sleep. For an instant, Nelly thought she might have imagined what she saw. Then, at that precise moment, there was a deafening crash from downstairs. The whole house shook to its very foundations.

Quinn O'Donnell sprung from his bed, put on his robe and ran towards the source of the sound. He could still hear the echo of the crash ringing in his ears as he dashed downstairs. On the ground floor, clouds of thick dust swirled along the corridors towards him. He arrived at the West Wing a few seconds later. When the dust finally began to settle, it was clear that the entire floor of the Great Orangery had collapsed, revealing a deep sink hole beneath it. It was as though Hell itself had torn Hogg Hall a brand-new arse. O'Donnell stood staring at the carnage; his jaw dropped. He was soon joined by Viscount Hatcher and Lady Labia Antoinette.

"Should I go and put the kettle on?" asked O'Donnell.

"I think that would be a very good idea," said Hatcher.

*

Next morning, in the Great Dining Room, the family were unusually quiet. There was a steaming pot of coffee and a plate of bacon sandwiches on the table, but no one was eating anything.

"I can't believe you slept through that crash!" said Hatcher to his father.

A strange look came over Hardy's face. "Last night I slept the sleep of the dead," he whispered, "and I dreamed the dread dreams of the long departed."

Viscount Hatcher topped up his coffee, his hand shaking very slightly. Lady Labia caught his eye as she tried to disguise a guilty pout.

"I went on a celestial journey," said Hardy, "and when I awoke this morning, I suddenly realised something very profound indeed."

"That you should stop drinking?" asked Lady Labia.

"Never going to happen," smiled Hardy, and he stood up dramatically. "I have made a decision," he announced, "it is time to stop fighting for Hogg Hall. The poor old girl has had enough. She is past repair. She is beyond rescue. This proud old house is no longer redeemable, and the day has dawned for the family to let her go."

Earl Hardy Hogg-Marchmont had finally accepted his fate, and the fate of Hogg Hall.

Chapter Five

Soon after breakfast, O'Donnell wished Countess Isabella many happy returns of the day. Her entire family had forgotten her birthday once again, as indeed she had herself, but at least her trusty servant had remembered. He always remembered.

"Thank you, O'Donnell," said the Countess. "Where is my husband?"

Deeply distressed by the imminent fate of Hogg Hall, Hardy had once again disappeared without trace.

"Has he gone fishing again?" asked Isabella.

"No, milady," O'Donnell replied. "I am afraid he has gone to the beach."

"Oh God," sighed the Countess. "Should we alert the authorities?"

The only thing more dangerous than a fishing trip to the lake, was when Hardy, Thornaby and Angus Ingleby-Barwick decided to go to the beach. Over the years, they had devised a number of sea/sand-related mischiefs, and whenever they headed off towards the sandy bay at

Muddleton Point, Isabella always knew they'd cook up some ill-conceived scheme that would land them in hot water with the local constabulary.

As usual, the Sixth Earl and his wingmen began their beano in the snug bar at the Pig & Pencil Case, where they conscientiously worked their way along the beer pumps on the bar. There were six pumps, each dispensing progressively stronger and more lethal local brews. There was Thumper's IPA, Thumper's Old Retainer and Thumper's Fat Monk, which was Melton's favourite. At the other end of the bar was Crotch Guzzler, Crotch Broadside, and a new brew called Crotch Embalmer, which had a specific gravity of 18.5 and was served with a printed health warning from Her Majesty's Government.

The merry band worked their way through these beers from left to right, and then back again in the opposite direction, sinking twelve pints each and then topping off the session with three quadruple cognacs, specially imported from Northern France by the landlord's brother-in-law Jacques, whose family had been smuggling contraband into Muddleton since 1832.

Satisfied that they were sufficiently lubricated, the trio set off for the beach, stopping only to pick up three Prime Potter's Pasties from Mrs. McGuffin's Bakery, opposite the head of the pier.

Muddleton Pier had been rebuilt many times. It had fallen down, burnt down, been washed away, been bombed by a German Zeppelin and had, on five occasions, been demolished in the fog by the same Norwegian oil tanker.

The Hogg-Marchmont family had also been

responsible for its destruction several times, including a Christmas morning collapse during an impromptu water polo tournament in 1873, and a mysterious explosion during an Easter egg hunt in 1901.

On this day, Hogg-Marchmont and his compadres were for once not targeting the pier. In fact, they were yet to decide on how they would entertain themselves on the golden sands. The tide was out, and several families had made camp on the beach. Colourful wind breaks, umbrellas and sun loungers dotted the scene, and everyone was relaxed and having a lovely time. The dark cloud that had threatened earlier was now disappearing out to sea, and a delightful blue sky made for a perfect English seaside setting. Even the not entirely attractive Muddleton Oil Rig, drilling a mile and a half offshore, glistened and gleamed in the sunlight.

Melton took three deckchairs from the promenade, and when the attendant asked him for £6, he simply showed the man his pimply bottom and marched onto the beach as if he owned it. It was Don Butcher's twentieth season as a deckchair attendant on Muddleton beach and he was fast losing the will to live. From an early age, Don had always wanted to be a lifeguard, and in preparation for this career path, he had learned the breaststroke, the crawl, the butterfly and the backstroke by the age of five. Unfortunately, when he applied to be a lifeguard at the age of eighteen, he discovered that he'd somehow completely forgotten how to swim, and no matter how hard he tried, he was unable to relearn that crucial skill.

A survey conducted in 2005 revealed that almost ninety-seven per cent of deckchair attendants are people who want to be lifeguards, but are unable to swim, and nearly all of them:

a) Have also forgotten how to ride a bike,
and/or

b) Show a number of suicidal tendencies.

It took Hardy a full twenty minutes to put up his deckchair, and as soon as he sat on it, it collapsed. Meanwhile, Ingleby-Barwick simply put his deckchair flat on the sand and fell face first onto it with a clump. Seeing the enticing, lustrous blue sea, Melton decided to go for a swim, and he removed his scarlet corduroys, revealing a rather grey and soiled pair of underpants, and a moth-eaten surgical truss. Luckily, on the way to the water's edge, he fell asleep on a groin, and the ocean was mercifully spared the wine critic's bodily pollutants.

Two hours later, after Hardy and his companions had all had an invigorating snooze, the Sixth Earl announced that it was time to play.

"I am going to build a sandcastle," he chimed.

"Good show!" cried Melton, and they all three scattered and began borrowing and stealing buckets and spades from nearby children on the beach. Hardy started digging first, and he was quickly joined by Ingleby-Barwick and Thornaby. The trio shovelled furiously, and they had soon created a hole large enough for Hardy to stand in, up to his waist.

Years before, in almost that identical spot, the group had once buried Hardy's son Hatcher up to his neck in sand, and not realising that the tide was coming in fast, they had wandered up to the Pig & Pencil Case for a pie and a pint. The water lapping around his face, Hatcher was rescued from drowning in the nick of time by a family of

Dutch tourists – a story that Hardy's son has since told many times whilst lying on a psychiatrist's couch.

Hardy, Melton and Angus dug frenziedly, and sand and pebbles flew everywhere. The hole was now roughly the size of a Ford Fiesta, and one or two passers-by were starting to pass comment.

"I thought we were supposed to be building a sandcastle," slurred the African.

"Bugger that," replied Hardy, "let's just dig the biggest fucking hole this beach has ever seen."

"Splendid wheeze," panted Melton.

"These kids' buckets and spades are not big enough," Hardy observed. "I'm going to the builder's merchants in the High Street to get some proper equipment."

Half an hour later, Hogg-Marchmont returned to the beach pushing a wheelbarrow crammed with shovels, spades, picks, buckets and an extendable ladder. He'd also stopped off at the off-licence and picked up two crates of Newcastle Brown Ale and a few litres of Famous Grouse.

Digging continued in earnest, and by late afternoon, the hole was about ten feet deep and twenty feet in diameter. Pink, sweating and fuelled by alcohol, Hardy and his friends were men possessed. If there was a world record for a hole on a beach, then they were surely going to break it. Thornaby dug so energetically at one point that his wig came off, and before he had an opportunity to pick it up and stick it back on his head, it was grabbed by a seagull.

"No!" screamed Thornaby, but he was too late. The bird was heading inland at speed, no doubt looking forward to adding this latest trophy to the other soft furnishings in its nest.

Melton lost so many toupees that he bought them in six packs from a wigmaker in East London, but this one was special – it had come to him in mysterious circumstances a decade before, and was the first time he had ever risked a ginger wig. Over the years, many people had commented on its chic and risqué style and hue. Since the late 1990s, Thornaby had mislaid over three hundred wigs, a large proportion of which were stolen by overzealous and mischievous birds.

Hardy and Angus were far too busy shovelling sand to notice Melton's pallid, naked scalp, and he quickly knotted the corners of his handkerchief and placed it on his head.

"What are you doing?" a muscly looking Australian shouted down at Hardy.

"Digging a hole!" the Sixth Earl yelled back at him.

"Fair enough," said the Australian. "Need any help?"

Hardy was momentarily torn. Another pair of hands would surely speed up the dig, but did he really want to share the credit for this magnificent enterprise?

"The more the merrier!" shouted Ingleby-Barwick taking control of the project, and the Australian jumped into the hole and began shovelling with his huge bare hands. 5pm came and went, and before long, ten or fifteen other beachgoers had gone and bought spades from the builders' merchant in the High Street and were digging on the beach. The crowd surrounding the hole was now swollen to three or four hundred, and some people began setting up barbecues and ferrying in cold boxes full of beer. The hole no longer belonged to Hardy Hogg-Marchmont – it belonged to the world.

As the sun got closer to the horizon, the excavation

was easily big enough to house two or three double-decker buses. A group of musicians set up nearby, and the crowd quickly swelled to over a thousand. Hardy, Angus and Melton were now far too drunk and exhausted to continue, but it didn't matter, as at least thirty people were now digging on the beach like their lives depended on it. The sand layer had been removed long ago, and the fittest members of the crowd were now using sharp, pointed pickaxes to break up the hard clay that lay below the gravelly soil and pebbles. As the light began to fade, people switched on their headlights in the car park, and the vast hole was bathed in light like an architectural dig. The landlord of the Pig & Pencil Case set up a makeshift bar on the beach, and there were soon hundreds of half-drunk villagers stumbling around on the promenade and the pier, which was now by far the best viewing platform to watch the unfolding drama on the sand.

"There's only solid rock now," said the Aussie to Hardy. "We can't dig any deeper!"

"Nonsense!" said the Sixth Earl, and he turned to Ingleby-Barwick. "Any ideas?" he asked.

Angus knew that it would be too dangerous to use explosives, so he needed to come up with something fast. Before he could think about it a second longer, there was a deafening bang, followed by a powerful gushing sound.

"Fuck me, we've struck oil!" screamed Hardy, as he spun around and saw a fountain of black gold pouring from the centre of his hole.

"Oh shit," sighed Ingleby-Barwick, "we've punched through the underground pipeline from the oil rig."

As the crowd cheered deliriously, the diggers jumped

clear, and the hole began to fill with thick, gloopy, crude oil. Soon there was a vast black lake in the middle of the beach.

"Better put out that cigar, old man," said Hardy to Thornaby.

"Good idea," said Melton, and he threw his Havana away. It took only a couple of seconds for the sea breeze to whisk it into the centre of the fast-growing lake of oil.

"Bugger!" said Hogg-Marchmont as the oil went up in a huge ball of flame, sending the screaming, terrified crowd scattering in all directions. There were around six hundred people on the pier, and as all six hundred of them simultaneously scattered in panic, the resulting vibration in the boardwalk caused the entire structure to crash into the sea.

"That fucking pier!" said Hogg-Marchmont.

"Cowboy builders," suggested Ingleby-Barwick.

"Time to scarper," whispered Melton Thornaby.

As the three friends belted like naughty schoolboys past the parish church, Hardy suddenly stopped dead in his tracks.

"Oh my God," he said.

"What is it, old man?" asked Melton.

"It's my wife's birthday!" whimpered the Sixth Earl.

"No problem," said Thornaby, and he clambered over the drystone wall of the churchyard and began filling his pockets with flowers from the graves.

Countess Isabella heard the explosion on the beach from the Great Dining Room at Hogg Hall. She calmly rose from the table and went and looked out of the window. There was a police helicopter hovering above the beach, from which an intense red glow could be seen emanating. She knew right away that whatever this was, it was her husband's doing.

Then there was a second, more distant and rumbling explosion, like that of an approaching storm. The Countess later learnt that this was the oil rig blowing up, the flames having travelled back along the pipeline and ignited its storage tanks.

"Shall I put the kettle on?" asked O'Donnell.

"Thank you," said the Countess.

Thirty minutes later, Hardy stood in the doorway of the Great Dining Room, clutching an impromptu bouquet of daffodils.

"Happy birthday," he said to the Countess.

*

The morning after their trip to the beach, Hogg-Marchmont and Ingleby-Barwick breakfasted late in the Great Dining Room. O'Donnell had laid out several trays of bacon, sausages and eggs, and there was also a generous supply of Muddleton Black Pudding which was officially the second blackest black pudding in the world, beaten only by Blackman's Black Country black pudding which was 2.8% blacker.

Hardy carefully scanned the local paper from the front page to the back page, but no matter how hard he tried, he could not find a single piece of news that was not in some way related to the explosion on the beach, the collapse of the pier and the complete destruction of Muddleton oil rig.

Casualties had been surprisingly light. The oil rig workers were on weekend leave, and most of the bathers on the beach were blown clear by the force of the blast. There were a few minor burns, a handful of broken limbs but only one actual death – that of a deckchair attendant called Don Butcher who it seemed had deliberately thrown himself into the conflagration.

"I enjoyed all that digging," said Thornaby.

"Yes, very therapeutic," echoed Ingleby-Barwick.

Hogg-Marchmont agreed. For some reason he did not yet understand, he had a feeling they would all be doing a lot more digging very soon.

Chapter Six

The monks from Ghastbury Abbey had been delivering their own special brand of elderberry wine to Hogg Hall since 1803. The monastery was just over ten miles away, and the brothers painstakingly rolled the barrels to Muddleton by hand, along the sodden dirt road that ran between the Velch and Spurn valleys. By the time they arrived, their hands were calloused and bleeding, and their feet were sore and blistered. The monks were, of course, delighted with these devotional injuries, and it was the main reason they made the journey. Hardy's usual order was twenty barrels, which meant that some of the brothers were forced to make two journeys, and the pain and discomfort of this ordeal brought them ever closer to the Lord.

Hardy was in the Great Sitting Room when he heard the wine arrive. He went and watched the monks solemnly roll the barrels through the Great Hall, then carry them one by one down the narrow, winding staircase to the vault. He liked the way he didn't have to make polite small talk with them, the brothers being a silent order who were only allowed to write, speak or think the word 'God'. This severely limited their conversation and made games of Scrabble at Ghastbury Abbey extremely short.

The monks had their own secret recipe, and sacred rituals, for making the wine. They would pick the elderberries by hand, then crush them with their feet while listening to Alanis Morissette. Then they'd pour the crushed berries into a huge copper pot with a hundred quarts of water and add thirty pounds of sugar, bringing the mixture to a slow simmer and turning off the heat. The juice was then poured into a fifty-gallon bathtub in the monks' latrine block, and while they were waiting for it to cool to room temperature, they would go outside into the cloisters, hitch up their habits and play Frisbee.

There was a special monk called Brother Tartaric, whose job it was to test the juice for acid and chuck in another ten or twenty pounds of sugar. He would also add something called pectic enzyme which he kept in a tiny glass vial attached to his belt. Three days later, the abbot would add a minute pinch of yeast nutrient and six bottles of tequila.

As soon as the delivery was complete, Hardy asked O'Donnell to fetch him a jug of the monks' latest batch from the cellar. It was a good year, sixty per cent proof and as sweet as cherry cola. As he sipped at the wine, he looked up forlornly at the Hogg-Marchmont coat of arms.

Designed by the First Earl just before his death in 1813, it consisted of four basic elements: the shield, the supporters, the crest and the motto. The shield was winged and divided into four quarters in which there were pictures of a goblet, a fork and spoon, a piece of stilton and a jar of pickled eggs. To the left and right of the shield were two rampant sows. On top, rested a gold coronet. The family motto was written in Latin underneath on an unfurling banner. It read *Unum In Via*.

"What does it mean?" Ingleby-Barwick once asked.

"Have One For The Road," replied Hardy proudly. The actual translation was 'One Way', but down the years, the Hogg-Marchmonts had put their own little spin on it.

Hardy's quiet study of the coat of arms was interrupted by a voice coming from near the doorway.

"Celestia May says she's just seen an angel in the library," it said. Hardy turned his head. It was Isabella.

"Back so soon?" he asked.

"We're both back," explained the Countess, "and as I said, Celestia May says she's just seen an angel in the library."

"Are you back for good?" asked Hardy.

Isabella ignored the question. "I asked her what type of angel it was," she continued, "and she said she wasn't sure."

"What types of angels are there?" asked Hardy, genuinely pleased to see his wife's face again.

"Oh, I don't know, archangels?" proffered Isabella.

"What are those little fat ones that look like babies?" asked Hardy.

"Cherubs?" suggested the Countess.

"Cherubim," corrected her daughter, and she trotted into the room and sat down on the right-hand facing Edwardian chaise longue.

"It's definitely not a cherubim," she said, "it's too tall."

"Does it have wings?" enquired Isabella.

"Of course it has wings," her daughter snapped. "It's an angel!"

"What's it doing here?" asked Hardy.

"How should I know?" said Celestia May.

"Well, did it say anything?" her father probed.

"No," said Celestia May.

"Is it still there now?" asked the Countess.

"I don't know, why don't you go and have a look!" said Celestia May sulkily, and she stomped out of the Great Sitting Room and scurried off along the corridor.

Countess Isabella eyed her husband. "I'm not going to sleep in the same room as you," she explained.

"Well, you have about eighty bedrooms to choose from," he said.

"Quite," said Isabella.

"I suppose we'd better go and see if that angel's still there," said Hardy, and the couple headed off towards the library. Celestia May often saw things. She saw ghosts; she saw pixies, and as far as she knew, she was the only practising white witch in Muddleton. She thought of herself as a soothsayer, a healer and a seer, although in her short lifetime, she had healed nothing at all and seen very little. She possessed no convictions for consorting with demons or weaving spells, and she remained pretty much undemonised by the people of the village. She'd never been put in the stocks, and she'd never been dunked into the river to see if she would float or sink.

Having read many books on the subject, Celestia May considered herself to be a mediator between the mundane world and the spiritual world, so for her, the more mundane the world was the better. In her dreams she contacted fairies, goblins, spirits and even the dead themselves. The girl had consorted with all six members of the Muddleton Morris Men, even old Ben Dunn, and she insisted that they wore their bell pads on their shins and waved their sticks and neckerchiefs in the air during congress.

She had also had several out-of-body experiences, one of which transported her to the top of the Great Folly and another which flew her economy class to Tenerife, losing her luggage on the way. As a card-carrying female divinity, Celestia May had advertised several times in the *Muddleton Gazette*, offering to teach magic, read Tarot cards and offer prophecies. Her only client thus far was a sixty-two-year-old widower with a toupee, who wanted to be 'cooked for and comforted physically'.

Celestia May began by worshipping the Moon Goddess, but more recently, she'd decided that she *was* the Moon Goddess. This mainly involved taking off her clothes and running around the grounds in the middle of the night. Around midnight, while he was closing the blinds in the kitchen, O'Donnell would often see her bony, naked body flash past the window, like one of the skeletons in *Jason and the Argonauts*.

At first, this activity would startle him, but now he'd got used to it and considered it simply part of the daily routine at Hogg Hall. On two occasions, he'd asked Celestia May what she was doing. The first time she replied that she was 'in pursuit of the Great Horned God', and on the second occasion she told him that the Great Horned God was in pursuit of her. O'Donnell derived from this that the pair took it in turns to chase each other, in some curious pagan game of tag.

Celestia May mainly used her witchcraft as an excuse to cut herself. Mind you, she didn't need much of an excuse to do that. Self-harm was now the hippest, coolest thing to do among young people in Muddleton, and many parents were now actively trying to get their children to start smoking cigarettes, rather than get hooked on this dangerous new addiction. Celestia May and her friends cut themselves, burnt themselves and even bit themselves almost every day. Then they'd all meet up together in casualty and chat about school and boys while the doctors stitched them up and bandaged their wounds. It was by far as popular as the ice rink and had now completely replaced roller disco. Even glue-sniffing and alcohol abuse was on the wane, and sales of razor blades had never been healthier. The kids were no longer doing it for attention; they were doing it for fun.

Celestia May was always an odd child. At the age of seven, her mother had once found her hovering three feet above her bed, her arms outstretched in the sign of the cross. The Countess had tried to talk her down, but her daughter had continued to float up there for almost two weeks. The family passed food up to her, they brought her changes of clothing, and sometimes Isabella even came into the room and read her a bedtime story. But her daughter stubbornly refused to stop levitating.

The ordeal finally came to a close when the Countess googled the problem and it was suggested that Celestia May should be fed a turnip. In desperation, Isabella tried this, and after only one bite of the vegetable, her daughter slowly floated back down onto the bed. Like a diabetic carries insulin, Celestia May now always kept a turnip in her bag, in case of unwanted levitation.

*

Mrs. Frapp gave Viscount Hatcher the most terrible glare as she passed him and Lady Labia in the Grand Hall.

"I saw you," she said, and she tottered her way towards the porch, to pick up a shopping delivery from Lidl. Hanging a couple of heavy baskets over her Zimmer frame, she set off towards the kitchen, muttering under her breath.

"What did she mean?" asked Labia, adjusting little Keith in his sling and patting his foul-smelling extremities.

"I have no idea," replied Hatcher, "I think she's getting a bit senile."

*

There was no angel in the library, which Hardy was quite disappointed about. He asked O'Donnell if anything else unusual had happened that morning.

"Unusual?" enquired the servant. "What kind of unusual?"

"Anything at all," shrugged Hardy.

"Celestia May said that there were five strange lights in the sky around dawn," he said.

"Oh, she's always seeing things," said Hogg-Marchmont.

"Can I do anything else for you, sir?" asked O'Donnell.

"No thanks," said the Sixth Earl. He went back to the Great Sitting Room and reacquainted himself with the monks' elderberry wine. After finishing the whole jug, Hardy dozed off and was awakened three hours later by Melton Thornaby.

"Ingleby-Barwick has started speaking in tongues," he announced.

"What's he saying?" asked Hardy.

"I don't know," shrugged Melton. "O'Donnell showed us into the library when we arrived, and Angus started speaking in tongues as soon as he got in there."

"There are some weird things happening in this house today," said Hardy, and he and Thornaby headed towards the library. Ingleby-Barwick was sitting bolt upright at the table, and O'Donnell was dabbing his forehead with a wet flannel and fanning his face with a copy of *Country Life*.

"*Et evolant ex inferno, et quinque comites*," said Ingleby-Barwick.

"Pardon?" asked Melton Thornaby.

"*Et evolant ex inferno, et quinque comites*," he repeated.

"Has he ever said anything like that before?" asked O'Donnell.

"Not as far as I know," said Melton.

"*Et evolant ex inferno, et quinque comites*," said Angus again and again, and a book suddenly flew off one of the top bookshelves and landed with a thud on the library floor.

"Is that his native language?" asked Hardy.

"What's his native language?" said Thornaby.

"I dunno, Swahili?"

"Sounds more like Latin," ventured Melton.

"I dropped out of Latin after one lesson!" admitted Hardy. "I didn't fancy the Latin teacher."

"*Et evolant ex inferno*," cried the African again, and he fell onto the floor with a thump.

"Help me get him up," said Hardy, and he and Melton picked up their friend and carried him over to the sofa.

His eyes suddenly flashed open. "*Et evolant ex inferno, et quinque comites*," he said, then he sat bolt upright and seemed to fully awake as if from a dream. "Whose leg do you have to hump to get a drink around here?" he said.

"Angus?" asked Hardy. "Are you OK?"

"Of course I'm OK," he replied, "but how in the holy name of Lembit Opik did I get here?"

"You were speaking in tongues," said Melton.

"What did I say?" asked Ingleby-Barwick.

"We don't know," said Hardy.

The Sixth Earl picked up the book that had flown from the top shelf. It was entitled *A Brief History of the Hogg-Marchmont Family*, and it had fallen open at the family tree.

"I think the house is talking to me," said Hardy.

Melton popped open a bottle of Mouton Cadet and poured three large glasses. O'Donnell served cheese and crackers and fetched some more wine from the cellar. Without warning, Countess Isabella could suddenly be heard screaming in the Great Sitting Room. The three men jumped to their feet and ran to the room next door. Isabella was on the chaise longue, her back arched, her loins trembling furiously. She let out another long, guttural scream, which Hardy recognised right away.

"What's wrong with her?" asked Ingleby-Barwick.

"There's nothing wrong with her," Hardy explained, "she's having an orgasm."

Countess Isabella stopped trembling, brushed her hair out of her face and sat up. "Oh dear, how very embarrassing," she said. "That's never happened before. One minute I was just sitting here quietly reading a magazine, and then the next minute... shazam."

"Shazam?" said Hardy.

"I think they call it a spontaneous orgasm," said Isabella, her neck flushing red. "It's not entirely uncommon."

"What on earth were you reading?" asked Ingleby-Barwick.

"A recipe for lasagne," replied the Countess.

"There are some very strange things going on in this house," observed Hogg-Marchmont again, and he and his companions returned to the library. Half a bottle of Mouton Cadet later, the screams from the Great Sitting Room started again, and there was a further occurrence about twenty minutes later.

Countess Isabella ran into the library. "Oh God, make it stop!" she pleaded.

"Try having a cold shower," suggested Melton.

"Why don't you just hold on and enjoy the ride?" said Hardy, who was now completely drunk and was beginning to find the whole thing a tad hilarious. Ingleby-Barwick googled it on his phone. "A woman from Atlanta," read Angus, "suffers from something called 'persistent sexual arousal syndrome'. It's also known as 'genital arousal disorder'."

Hardy sniggered like a Year 10.

"It's not funny," said Angus. "This woman in Atlanta

climaxes hundreds of times a day. She has to constantly exercise control over her body. She doesn't know if she's coming or going."

As Ingleby-Barwick continued to read, Countess Isabella could again be heard screeching with pleasure in the room next door.

"What's the cure?" asked Melton.

"There's no cure," said Angus. "It just says take an aspirin."

Isabella went off again, the loudest and longest one so far, this time banging on the floor as she reached conclusion.

"That was a big one," said Ingleby-Barwick, and he passed around the cigars.

"What the Hell is that noise?" shouted Viscount Hatcher as he bounded into the library. "It sounds like someone's being murdered down here!"

"Your mother is having spontaneous orgasms," slurred Hardy.

"Uggghhh," said Hatcher, as if someone had just force-fed him a lemon. "That's the most revolting thing I've ever heard."

The Viscount was of the firm belief that anyone who continued to enjoy any kind of sexual activity after the age of forty-five was some kind of twisted deviant. The fact that his mother had a clitoris at all was utterly disgusting to him. The walls shook, and the Great Bohemian Chandelier rattled as Countess Isabella's genitalia exploded again.

"For God's sake, Mother!" Hatcher yelled at the wall.

"She can't help it," said Melton, "it's a syndrome."

Hardy went into the Great Sitting Room. His wife was crossed-legged on the floor, an ice pack clamped on her front bottom.

"I blame you for this," she hissed.

"How is this my fault?" asked the Sixth Earl. "I'm not even in the room!"

"It's obviously some kind of medical condition that's been brought about by shock," the Countess reasoned. Hardy put his arm around his wife, and she came. He quickly took his arm away and she came again.

"I'll leave you to it," he said quietly, and he tiptoed back to the library. Thornaby and Ingleby-Barwick were now placing bets on when the Countess's vagina would next activate.

"I really don't think you should be gambling on this," said Hardy firmly, and as the next shriek came from the Great Sitting Room, Melton handed a crisp £20 note to Ingleby-Barwick, and the Sixth Earl placed a bet on when the next event would occur.

Nanny Alice came into the library holding Master Keith. "Is everything alright?" she asked.

Hardy had now drunk enough to feel flirty. With a nod, a wink and a revolting leer, he beckoned Alice into the room and invited her to take a seat by the mantelpiece. "Everything's fine," he assured her. "My wife is just a little overexcited today. I'm sure it's the thrill of becoming a grandmother."

The nanny sat down, and Hardy loomed over her, breathing foul and noxious gases in her general direction. "Would you like a drink, my dear?"

In the manner that only Mormons and recovering

alcoholics respond to that question, Nanny Alice snapped a rapid response. "I don't drink," she said.

Hardy took in her thick, dark brown woolly tights and her tightly buttoned blue cardigan. He had seen this look many times on NaughtyNannies.com.

Alice sniffed at the air suspiciously. "There's a lot of smoke in this room," she observed, and she sprang to her feet. "This is not a healthy environment for the baby," she said and left immediately, her flat shoes *slap, slapping* on the floorboards.

"Fine woman," said Melton Thornaby.

"I saw her first," growled Hogg-Marchmont.

*

Strange things were also happening that evening in the beehive under O'Donnell's bed. Bees are very sensitive to unusual vibes and negative forces, and this will often cause them to behave in erratic or unexpected ways. The worker bees were performing their usual waggle dance – a figure of eight pattern followed by a turn to the right. The direction and duration of this routine depends on what the bee is trying to communicate, and this activity is a fairly regular occurrence in bee circles. The drones, however, were doing something rather unusual. Not wishing to join in with the waggle dance, they had formed themselves into long columns and were line dancing while humming the tune of 'Achy Breaky Heart'.

Meanwhile, a large group of field bees were swarming around the queen and trying to impress her by playing air guitar and singing 'Wild Thing' by the Troggs. This may sound impressive but unfortunately, very few of them knew the correct lyrics.

Little Anthogrid's legs were now fully formed, and he was dying to join in with the dancing, but one of the nurse bees pulled him roughly back into the brood chamber. But Anthogrid was a free spirit, and he soon began line dancing on his own as the bees in the next chamber joined in with the country stylings of Billy Ray Cyrus. It was clear that Anthogrid was destined for great things.

*

Hardy could not get to sleep that night. He tossed and he turned as the mystifying events of the day went around and around in his head. Ingleby-Barwick was no longer speaking in tongues and was fast asleep in the Queen of Scots Bedroom.

After four and a half hours, the Countess had finally stopped having orgasms and had retired, exhausted, to bed. But Hardy kept thinking about the curious lights that Celestia May had seen in the sky. Slowly sobering up, his hangover fast approaching, the Sixth Earl put on his dressing gown and quietly let himself out of the front door. It's hard to walk quietly over a crunchy, gravel drive, but Hardy did his best. He didn't want to wake the house. He looked up at the astronomical clock, and it told him that the moon had just entered its waning phase, which he didn't really need to know. He just wanted to know the time.

The yellowing, marble statue of Polyclitus gave him a nasty look as he crept past. This naked, Greek statue always gave Hardy the skunk eye, and he hated the sight of it. He could, however, console himself in the knowledge that the subject of this ancient piece still had an intact penis, but its hands had both broken off.

For once at Hogg Hall, it was a clear, cloudless night. With the key he kept on a chain around his neck, Hogg-Marchmont unlocked the observatory with a satisfying click and went inside. It was freezing cold. Leaving the lights switched off, he wound the wooden handle that opened the shutters on the domed roof, revealing the gently revolving canopy of stars above. Hardy tugged at a dust sheet, and as it fell seductively to the floor, it revealed the Sixth Earl's pride and joy: a sixteen-inch Newtonian reflecting telescope, beautifully balanced on a heavy equatorial mount, with quartz-controlled drive motors.

Hogg-Marchmont ran his hands up and down the barrel of the device, then he suddenly grasped hold of it and tilted it upwards towards the sky. With this magnificent tool, Hardy had explored craters on Mars, stars in Orion's Belt and the satellites of Jupiter. He'd tracked comets, glimpsed shooting stars and marvelled at the rings of Saturn. He was about to get his bearings by rotating the mount towards Polaris, when something caught his eye in the northern sky. Five yellowish lights were moving slowly across the heavens, in the approximate direction of Hogg Hall. They weren't aircraft, they were moving too slowly, and they were far too rapid to be any kind of distant astronomical body.

"Well, I'll be darned," breathed Hardy softly, and he adjusted the telescope to point directly at one of the lights. A fair amount of refocusing was required as the objects were clearly not more than a few miles away. The lights appeared to be flying in a delta formation, and the object in the centre suddenly pulled into sharp focus. It was a man. Hardy lurched away from the viewfinder and blinked his eyes tightly three or four times. Then he looked again. Sure enough, the telescope revealed a middle-aged man in a white, powdered wig. He was dressed in a long, velvet robe, trimmed around the edges with heraldic ermine fur, and across his breast he sported a scarlet, silken sash. He was carried aloft by his own immense pair of bird's wings – perhaps those of an Andean condor or an albatross, and he glowed as brightly and as warmly as the setting sun.

From his portrait in the Great Sitting Room, Hardy knew this man's face well. It was Waldegrave Hogg-Marchmont, First Earl of Hogg Hall. Hardly daring to breath, Hardy panned the telescope to the left. Flying alongside the First Earl was a handsome gentleman in a black tunic with a high collar – his throat tightly wrapped in a crisp, white neckerchief. It was Jellico Rivers Hogg-Marchmont, the Second Earl. These five angelic beings were the five previous Earls of Hogg Hall, which meant that one of the formation must surely be Hardy's father. He panned the telescope to the right, to reveal Third Earl, Waldrup Hogg-Marchmont, resplendent in a winged collar, three-quarter-length grey jacket and top hat. Flying just behind the Third Earl's port wing was Kenneth Hogg-Marchmont, hero of the Luftwaffe and the Fourth Earl. He was clad in flying helmet, goggles and a black leather bomber jacket, and he dipped his wings in true fighter pilot fashion as the formation soared over the Great Folly, then rapidly reduced altitude and banked south-eastwards towards the front of the house.

Moments later, there was a deafening beating of wings as the Earls came in for a landing on the gravel drive, a huge cloud of dust thrown into the air as they touched down. Hardy rushed out of the observatory and there, in the semi-darkness, five glowing figures stood side by side. The dust finally settled, and the figure on the far left of the formation stepped forward. Sure enough, it was Sidney Hogg-Marchmont, the Fifth Earl of Hogg Hall and Hardy's late father. Hardy stood frozen to the spot, and his father walked calmly towards him, his wings folding back neatly.

"Was it you that Celestia May saw in the library?" asked Hardy.

The Fifth Earl smiled. "Yes, it was me," he said. "We came down here yesterday for a recce. She didn't recognise me. She was very young when I went away."

The Fifth Earl moved close to his son. He stroked the hair on his cheek. "Your daughter really needs to eat something," he said.

"I need a drink!" announced the First Earl, and he paraded off towards the library, his gown dragging on the driveway. He may have died of liver failure at the age of fifty, but now he had a serious thirst on. He'd helped plan Hogg Hall in 1792, so he knew his way to the wine cellar.

"No wait, I've got a few decent bottles of claret in the observatory," said Hardy, and the five Earls wasted no time at all in piling inside. Once they had all entered the tiny building, the celestials appeared much more human. Within half an hour, everyone was pissed, and there was much laughter and testosteroned beating of wings.

"Did your handsome wife enjoy my attentions yesterday?" the First Earl asked Hardy. "They didn't call me silver tongue for nothing."

"You old goat," said the Third Earl, and he punched his grandfather heartily on the shoulder.

"Our coming was foretold," said the Second Earl. "Your brown friend Ingleby-Barwick was given a message to deliver."

"I think it got a little garbled in translation," said Hardy. "What language was he speaking?"

"It was the tongue of Diablo," roared the First Earl, "but I'm afraid he didn't speak it very well. You're supposed to put the verb at the end of the sentence."

Hardy was having a little trouble taking all this in. He opened a second bottle of claret and topped up everyone's glasses.

"What's all this nonsense about Hogg Hall being demolished?" asked the Second Earl, Jellico Rivers.

"Yes," replied Hardy, a little embarrassed by the question, "I'm afraid it looks like the old place has finally given up the ghost."

"Absolute rubbish!" boomed Waldrup, the Third Earl. "They've been telling us this place needs pulling down since the mid-nineteenth century. Tell the buggers to go and boil their heads!"

The Fourth Earl, meanwhile, seemed more interested in the telescope than in the debate about the future of Hogg Hall. "It's a sixteen-inch reflector, isn't it?" he noted, with the sharp observational skills of a pilot. "I always wanted one of these."

"You cannot stand by and allow the destruction of

Hogg Hall," Sidney told his son. He knew that laws were made to be broken, and proclamations made to be ignored.

"Sorry, I've made up my mind," insisted Hardy. "They can tear the place down any time they want. It's over."

"It's not your decision, boy!" grunted the First Earl, his face ablaze with anger. "Hogg Hall does not belong to you! It belongs to all of us!"

"You need to grow some balls, my lad," roared the Third Earl, his top hat shuddering with displeasure. Waldrup was a fierce and vigorous man. He'd died on top of a whore at the age of eighty, and he was in no mood to take prisoners.

Just before dawn, Celestia May was awakened by what she thought was the beating of wings. An amber glow was coming from outside, and when she went to the window, she saw that it was coming from the observatory. Barefooted, she climbed from her window and used her favourite drainpipe to clamber down into the courtyard. It took only a few seconds for her to skip and run from the house to the lake. A dragonfly skimmed across the water, tentatively testing its new wings.

Celestia May stood outside the observatory and noticed that the domed roof was wound open. She could hear voices inside, and she peeped through the window.

The Second Earl, a renowned explorer and womaniser, who'd died of both malaria and syphilis in 1873, felt that it was now time to make a rousing speech. The hairs on his cheeks bristled, as did those of every Hogg-Marchmont in the room.

"How do we judge a man?" he asked. "A good citizen? A good husband? A good father? Well, I was none of those buggering things. I was not honest in my dealings with other men; I was unfaithful to my wife; and for most of my life, I had an unsound mind in an unsound body."

The Hogg-Marchmonts cheered heartily, for this was surely their manifesto. Hardy suddenly wished that his son Hatcher was there to hear it. The late Second Earl took a slug of claret and continued, his wings beating powerfully behind him, his gloved fist raised in the air. "In a free country we must be willing to take up arms for the defence of our lands, our property and our homes! Cry God, Hardy and Hogg Hall!"

"Hoorah!" cried the five Earls, and all at once, the sunrise threw a long ribbon of soft peach-coloured light into the room.

"You won't let me down, will you, son?" whispered Sidney in the Sixth Earl's ear.

Hardy looked at his father. "OK, I'll do what I can," he said, and before he knew it, the five Earls were gone. This was the fifth time the Sixth Earl had said a final farewell to his father. The first time he'd no way of knowing the significance of the moment, as it was the last time he spoke to his father before he died.

"I'll see you tomorrow," he'd said, and he gave his elderly father a firm handshake. The second farewell was at the hospital. The doctor had just told him that the Fifth Earl would never regain consciousness, and Hardy gently held his sleeping father's hand and said goodbye while an insensitive nurse clattered around the ward collecting cups and plates. The third farewell was at Muddleton crematorium as the curtains slowly closed around Sidney's coffin, and the fourth was three days later as he and the

Countess scattered his father's ashes in woodland behind the Great Folly. Naturally, Hardy thought that that would be his final farewell to the Fifth Earl, but now his father was soaring upwards into the firmament, the morning sky adorned with a grim, shepherd's warning of towering crimson clouds.

"Goodbye again," said Hardy, and he walked back to Hogg Hall. But would that fifth farewell really be the last?

*

On the day his father's ashes were sprinkled near the Great Folly, Hardy went for a restorative walk in the north woods, and a few hundred yards from the lake, he stumbled upon an outbuilding that had never been there before. A small, wooden, six-sided shed had manifested itself. It had an ornate turret and a stout metal grill on all six sides. Sitting inside the structure, its claws clamped around a thick rustic perch, was a majestic peregrine falcon. An impressive, crow-sized bird, the falcon sported a blue-grey back, barred white underparts and a jet-black head. It blinked slowly and turned its head to look at Hogg-Marchmont.

"Where the Hell did you come from?" said Hardy under his breath, and the mood of that sad day changed almost instantly to one of wonder and awe.

The peregrine is typical of bird-eating raptors, females being considerably larger than males. This was surely a female. As their eyes met, the Sixth Earl felt sure that the pair must have encountered one another before, perhaps in a previous life. The falcon flicked her savagely hooked beak flirtily upwards and spread her tail feathers wide. The peregrine is renowned for its speed, reaching over 200mph during its characteristic hunting stoop, making it the fastest member of the animal kingdom, and Hardy knew that the highest measured speed of a peregrine falcon was 242mph. He'd seen it on *Blue Peter*.

The Sixth Earl carefully opened one of the doors in the grill and *falco peregrinus* stepped onto his outstretched arm and allowed him to remove her from the falconry.

"I shall call you Boudicca," he said to the bird, and she immediately beat her wings and took to the air. The creature circled three times in the clearing above his head, then shot like a missile out over the treetops and disappeared into the late afternoon gloom.

"Well, that was short and sweet," muttered Hardy, and he felt an immediate sense of loss at the thought that he might never see the bird again. Ten minutes later, the Sixth Earl turned and headed back towards the house, but after he'd taken only a couple of steps, he heard a dull thud on the ground behind him. He spun around, and there, on the forest floor, was the body of a plump wood pigeon. A gift from Boudicca.

Hogg-Marchmont stretched out his hand. The falcon swooped down like a fighter aircraft and, with a whoosh of air and frantic fluttering of wings, settled back on his forearm.

"Pigeon for dinner," smiled Hardy. He picked the limp prey up off the ground and, like old friends, he and the peregrine headed for Hogg Hall.

Boudicca perched serenely on the mantelpiece as Hardy, Melton and Angus tucked into roast pigeon that evening, and the only topic of conversation was the falcon. The recent demise of the Fifth Earl was hardly mentioned at all. Such is the attention span of the nobility. Celestia May and Countess Isabella came into the room. "You cannot keep that creature in the house," she insisted, "it's unhygienic."

"It's more hygienic than Melton Thornaby," said Celestia May.

She held out her arm. The falcon quickly settled on her, and within moments, it was taking pieces of food from her mouth. She had a way with birds of prey and had once, at the tender age of four, miraculously kept both a kestrel and a field mouse as pets.

"While its diet consists almost exclusively of medium-sized birds, the peregrine will occasionally hunt small mammals," Thornaby read from his phone. "Let's take it hunting," he said.

The following morning, the three companions headed for the north woods, the falcon sat proudly on Hardy's arm. The Sixth Earl knew nothing of falconry, but then he had never been one to over-research anything. Melton passed around his hip flask, which was much too large to be worn on the hip. Indeed, it was so big it sometimes had to be wheeled through the undergrowth on a small gun carriage.

"What happens now?" asked Ingleby-Barwick, and as if in answer, the peregrine fanned out its wings and its tail feathers and took off.

"I suppose we just wait here until the creature returns with a rabbit or two," replied Hardy. The trio sat down on a log and set about the serious task of getting squiffy. An hour passed, and then another.

"Falconry is not all it's cracked up to be, is it?" commented Ingleby-Barwick, and at that instant, there was a loud beating of wings and Boudicca dropped a dead sheep onto the ground in front of them.

"Now that's what I call a falcon!" bawled Melton Thornaby.

Hardy eyed the fat, woolly prey before them. "Fuck me, who knew a falcon could take a sheep?" he said.

Strange things like this tended to happen quite a lot to Hardy Hogg-Marchmont, and you either went with them or you didn't. Much of the time, the laws of physics did not seem to apply at Hogg Hall. Before Hardy could reward the bird, it took off again and rocketed into the distance above the trees. The rear leg of the sheep twitched.

"It's not dead," whispered Ingleby-Barwick.

"Don't worry, I'll finish it off," said Hogg-Marchmont, and he pulled out his trusty fishing pistol and put a bullet neatly between the poor creature's eyes.

"The farmer will have my bollocks for sweetmeats if he finds out about this," hissed Hardy. "We'll have to bury the fucker."

"No," said the African, ever resourceful. "We'll fill it with stones and push it into the river."

An hour and a half later, the three reached the riverbank, sweating and exhausted from their labours.

"Perhaps we should have moved it before we filled it with stones," said Hardy, and they rolled the sheep into the River Turd. It quickly sank without trace, leaving a little circle of bubbles on the surface.

Hogg Hall was playing with time like a child plays with plasticine, stretching and rolling and moulding it into mystifying new shapes, and this was just the beginning. The peregrine turned to Hardy and spoke. "One day, you too shall fly," it said, "just like your father, and his ancestors before him."

"What does that even mean?" Hardy asked the bird.

"All will be revealed," said Boudicca, and she launched herself into the air and was never seen again. The next time Hardy looked, the falconry in the woods had vanished.

Chapter Seven

Melton Thornaby awoke in the Queen of Scots Bedroom around 7am, his mouth dry, his head pounding like it always did when he first regained consciousness from the inky void. He slid off the four-poster bed, and wearing nothing but his tartan cashmere socks, he padded his way to the Great En-Suite Bathroom. Most of his urine missed the toilet bowl and promptly soaked into an Arabesque Beige Rug. His bottom spoke, and as a precaution, he wiped it with a piece of three-ply toilet paper. It wasn't until Melton climbed back into bed that he noticed that Mrs. Frapp was there. She was fast asleep.

Melton peeked under the covers. She was naked. There was an unclad, ninety-year-old woman in his bed – her clothes neatly folded on an armchair, and her Zimmer parked next to the bow-fronted chest of drawers by the window. On the walnut cabinet beside the bed, there was a glass tumbler in which a set of yellow dentures floated serenely.

Melton dry-retched into his hand. Had the old lady taken advantage of his inebriated state and forced herself upon him? Or had he perhaps mistaken her for someone else, and copulated with her erroneously? Maybe he'd simply got into the wrong bed. Should Thornaby wake her up? Or should he sneak out of the room, like a cad and a bounder? A million questions went through his head, and then the door opened suddenly, and O'Donnell came into the room, carrying a silver tray with a pot of tea and a cup and saucer on it. Melton quickly pulled the covers over Mrs. Frapp's head.

"Should I open the curtains, sir?" asked the servant, as he poured the tea.

"No thank you," replied Melton.

"Very well," said O'Donnell, and he began to remove himself from the room. As he did so, Mrs. Frapp awoke with a start and opened her eyes. Her face being unexpectedly under the sheets, she immediately thought she'd gone blind during the night and screamed.

O'Donnell stopped in his tracks and turned to face the bed. He was greeted by the sight of Mrs. Frapp's head popping up from behind the duvet.

"I can explain," whimpered Melton Thornaby.

"I'm quite sure you can, sir," said O'Donnell. "Will there be anything else?"

"No thank you," replied Melton, and the servant left, closing the door rather more loudly than usual.

Nelly Frapp had been doing this all her life. She would prey upon visitors to Hogg Hall by waiting until they were drunk, and then silently crawling into bed with them while they were asleep. Her motives were not sexual. She would simply wait until her victims awoke, and then suggest that they had tampered with her. Then she'd ask them for £10 to keep quiet.

Melton was constantly drunk at Hogg Hall and was often forced to sleep over. Mrs. Frapp was able to con him on a fairly regular basis, because his short-term memory was failing fast, and he therefore had the recall of an ageing goldfish. No matter how many times it happened, Thornaby would experience little more than a vague feeling of déjà vu, and would pay the old lady without question. Nelly usually awoke around 5am and roused her befuddled victim. She would express her consternation, collect her money and creep out of the room before the rest of the house awoke. But with the best will in the world, Mrs. Frapp was now getting a little old for this racket, which is why, on this fateful occasion, she had overslept for the first time in seventy years and been discovered in bed with Melton.

*

"A duel?" exclaimed Hogg-Marchmont. "You can't challenge Melton Thornaby to a duel!"

O'Donnell remained calm. "He has defiled the honour of a lady," insisted the servant.

"I'm sure there is a perfectly good explanation," said Hardy, and he put his hand onto O'Donnell's shoulder and patted it warmly.

"I shall challenge Mr. Thornaby after breakfast," said the servant.

Hogg-Marchmont confronted Melton in the Great

Library, where he discovered his friend medicating himself with a large Bloody Mary. He immediately asked him if he had probed the old lady.

"Possibly," said Melton.

"Jesus, Mary and Joseph, man, she's ninety years old!" yelled Hardy.

The Sixth Earl looked his friend square in the eye. "O'Donnell is going to challenge you to a duel," he said.

"A duel?" retorted Melton. "What do you mean, a duel?"

"There is a long tradition of duelling at Hogg Hall," Hardy told Thornaby. "If O'Donnell demands satisfaction, you will be obligated to use the John Twigg Pistols. They were owned by the First Earl and have taken the lives of many a foolish man at Hogg Hall."

"You can't be serious," pleaded Melton. "I don't know how to shoot a flintlock pistol!"

Hardy took a small key out of a drawer and used it to unlock the wooden cabinet below. He removed a mahogany case and put it on the table. Melton opened it. Inside were a pair of silver mounted flintlock duelling pistols with twenty-three-bore, eight-inch, twist-sighted barrels. The metal was profusely engraved, and the handles beautifully carved with the Hogg-Marchmont coat of arms. Alongside the pistols, was a red leather powder flask.

"They still have the original ramrods," smiled Hardy, and he ran his hand along one of the barrels.

"I am not going to duel with your servant," said Melton, but he could already see that he might have little choice.

The traditional duelling ground at Hogg Hall was in a small clearing in the woodland behind the lake, about two hundred yards from the Great Folly. Hundreds of duels had taken place there over the centuries, but the most renowned was probably in 1789. Prince Ferdinand Butt-Vanguard, Duke of Hertford, challenged Lieutenant-Colonel Charles Montague-Crabb, having accused him of making 'certain noises unworthy of a gentleman'. Montague-Crabb had no recollection of making any such noises, but the Prince's demands for an apology were refused. Butt-Vanguard demanded satisfaction, and the two men met with pistols on Christmas Day. According to a report in the *Muddleton Gazette*, Butt-Vanguard's shot 'grazed his opponent's forehead'. Montague-Crabb, however, refused to fire back, stating that he had been called out to give satisfaction to the Prince, and that satisfaction had been given. Butt-Vanguard refused to accept that honour had been satisfied and insisted that the Lieutenant-Colonel shoot him. Stalemate was reached, and the two men stood and faced each other long into the night.

Next morning, the pair were still at the duelling ground, and Butt-Vanguard continued to wait for Montague-Crabb's shot. It began to snow. Six hours later, a blizzard having engulfed them, both men died of exposure. To this day, the Butt-Vanguard family still demand to be shot at by the Montague-Crabbs every Christmas.

*

As soon as Melton Thornaby had finished eating his scrambled egg and Cumberland sausages, O'Donnell politely asked if he would stand up.

"I demand satisfaction!" insisted the servant, and taking a leather glove from his pocket, he slapped Thornaby hard around the face.

"Tomorrow morning at dawn," he said.

"What time is that?" asked Melton.

"Around 5am," replied the servant.

"Look, old man, I'm not really a morning person," said Thornaby, "I don't suppose we could shift it to tomorrow afternoon?"

O'Donnell raised his eyebrows. "How about 2pm?" he said. Melton wondered if that would be enough time for him to have a long lunch and get good and plastered first.

"Three o'clock?" he asked.

"Very well," said the servant. "Three o'clock at the duelling ground behind the lake. Shall I bring the pistols, or will you?"

"You bring the pistols," said Thornaby, "and I'll bring a bottle."

O'Donnell picked up Melton's empty plate from the table and strode from the Great Dining Room.

Quinn O'Donnell was a proud man. He was born in Dublin in 1947, and his family background was what some like to call 'shabby genteel'. O'Donnell's parents were strict Catholics, and he was an active member of the Saint Mary the Virgin Choir, where he was invited on numerous occasions to what Father Connor liked to call his 'Sausage Surgeries'.

O'Donnell's father, a hotel manager, died when he was just six, leaving a wife and twenty-six children. As a child, Quinn suffered from poor eyesight, a condition which the priest convinced him was brought about by not masturbating enough. The problem with his vision interfered greatly with his early education, but O'Donnell managed to teach himself to read and write by the time he was thirteen.

Quinn left school at fourteen and worked at a variety of jobs, including potato boiler, egg breaker, cow puncher, worm picker and snake milker. Then he had three years in the army, followed by a brief period as a farmhand. He was sacked from that job for not taking off his cap while collecting his wage packet.

O'Donnell worked in a hotel for a while and then as an assistant manager in a Dublin restaurant. He moved to England at the age of twenty-nine and answered an advertisement to be Butler to the Fifth Earl, Sidney Hogg-Marchmont. O'Donnell barely knew what a butler was, but his extensive knowledge of Irish whiskeys, horse racing and arms smuggling greatly impressed the Fifth Earl. Before he knew it, he both lived and worked at Hogg Hall.

In the early days, Nelly Frapp was a great mentor to O'Donnell, schooling him in the intricacies of life in service. He always admired Nelly, and perhaps, when she was a younger woman, he had even been a little in love with her. Mrs. Frapp also clearly had a great deal of respect for Mr. O'Donnell, as she'd never once waited for him to get drunk, crept into bed with him and then asked him for £10.

Traumatised by the events of that morning, O'Donnell went and had a lie-down in his room, and he was comforted by the gentle humming of the bees under his bed.

*

Deep inside the hive, Anthogrid was growing up fast. The life of a bee being only a few days, he was already a teenager, and was ready to go out on his first forage for pollen. Arvid and Egil collected him from his hexagonal cell, and the three clambered to the entrance of the hive.

Anthogrid peeked outside. "The world is very big, isn't it?" he said nervously.

"This isn't the world," replied Arvid. "This is just a single bedroom. Wait until you see outside the house."

Anthogrid took off shakily, and the two other bees led him towards the open window. Arvid and Egil slipped skilfully through the gap between the frame and the wall, but Anthogrid flew straight into the glass. This was, of course, the first rite of passage of all first-time foragers from the hive.

Arvid turned around and hovered as Anthogrid flew again and again into the window pane.

"Shall I go and get him?" suggested Egil.

"Nah, let him learn his lesson," smiled Arvid, and the pair watched as the little bee smashed his head repeatedly into the glass, just as they had done on their first outing.

An hour later, Egil flew back inside and helped to guide Anthogrid towards the gap. His head was swollen and painful, and he was experiencing double vision.

In the gentle drizzle that almost always engulfed Hogg Hall, the three bees flew across the north courtyard and downwards towards the flowers that grew at the lake.

"Now what do I do?" asked Anthogrid.

Egil helped him land on a bright, lemon iris. "Sit on that," he said.

Through the power of static electricity, Anthogrid could feel his entire body begin to attract pollen grains. He felt the hairs on his legs stiffen and the pollen start to accumulate on his thighs.

"Now stick your tongue in there," said Arvid.

The young bee had never tasted anything so good as he sucked hungrily on the sugary nectar inside the flower. If he'd known what sex was, he would probably have said that this was better. He experienced his first sugar buzz. He felt high on life, and then... he sneezed.

"What was that?" screamed Egil.

It turned out Anthogrid was the first bee in history to suffer from hay fever.

*

No one had ever seen the Beast in the Woods, but everyone knew it was there. As early as 1805, Earl Waldegrave Hogg-Marchmont reported seeing footprints, as large as twenty-four inches long, in the wet clay on the north bank of the lake. He wrote in his diary of an 'omnivorous and mainly nocturnal beast whose habitat appears to be the grounds of Hogg Hall and who has extremely large feet'.

When he was in his twenties, Hardy had once been sunbathing near the lake, and had heard something very large moving through the trees and growling like a lion. He also reported a strong, unpleasant smell, similar to that which comes from the kitchens of Harvester restaurants.

The Third Earl claimed many times to have seen what he described as a large, hairy, bipedal humanoid, and wrote that it stole his top hat one Thursday afternoon in March. He went on to say that the Beast was exceedingly tall and covered in reddish hair. A police artist who later worked with the Third Earl sketched immense round eyes, a pronounced brow ridge and a large, low-set forehead.

In the 1940s, the Fourth Earl was once roughly assaulted by a 'giant, hairy, muscular man' while returning home late one night. Since it is well known that he would regularly pay good money for such entertainment in London, this sighting is rarely taken seriously.

Around the same time, the Beast was reported to have attacked the Muddleton Morris Men, during an unscheduled late-night performance outside the Pig & Pencil Case. They managed to beat him off with their wooden staffs, but Mr. Cribbage sustained a nasty bite on his left buttock.

It should be said that local zoologists completely discount the existence of this creature, considering it to be a combination of folklore, misidentification and overactive imagination. There is certainly a lack of physical evidence and no indication at all of the large numbers of these creatures that would be necessary to maintain a breeding population over many hundreds of years.

Occasional new reports of sightings sustain a small group of self-described Beast Spotters, who meet in the pub every Tuesday evening and organise vigils by the lake. They take night-vision binoculars, infrared cameras and a disposable barbecue.

Many recent so-called sightings of the Beast have been shown to be hoaxes. In 2014, Bruce Langsman, a regular from the Pig & Pencil Case, appeared on the breakfast show on Muddleton FM and announced that he was 'ninety-eight per cent sure' that he could capture the Beast of Hogg Hall.

It should be mentioned here that Muddleton FM had very little credibility. The station operated on an extremely low budget, and their aggressively rotated playlist consisted of just six records, all of them by Kid Creole and the Coconuts.

A month later, Langsman announced on the same show that he had the Beast tied up in the back of a Ford Transit van and that people could come and see it if they bought a ticket. After collecting almost £9,000 via PayPal, he announced on Twitter that the creature had escaped, and before anyone could ask him for a refund, he disappeared without trace.

In 2015, a Muddleton man was run over by a car, while perpetrating a hoax using a gorilla suit hired from the theatrical costumiers Angels.

*

"I have changed my mind," announced Hogg-Marchmont. He had gathered the family in the Great Sitting Room and was clearly in a determined mood. "I'm not giving up on Hogg Hall after all," he said, "I'm going to fight the council over the demolition."

"What brought that on?" asked Isabella, not sure whether to be happy or sad.

"What nonsense," said Lady Labia Antoinette, her baby wriggling and making smells reminiscent of a medieval sewer. "A couple of days ago you were ready to drive the bulldozer yourself!"

"We have a sacred duty to our ancestors," said Hardy.

"What utter bull crap!" screamed his son. "Knock the fucker down and sell the land. There's enough room here to build a small town."

"Hogg Hall is not ours to sell," said Hardy, thumping the mantelpiece and sending a small bronze statue of Wellington flying. "It belongs to history. It belongs to England. It is an architectural jewel!"

He hammered the mantel shelf again, and this time one of the tiles fell off, and a dead pigeon plopped from the chimney and landed in the hearth.

Hardy marched into the centre of the Great Sitting Room. "I have a plan," he said. "I'm going to set up a fighting fund and raise enough money to bribe the mayor."

"Oh dear," said Isabella, "here we go again."

"Who is the mayor?" asked Hardy. He normally took very little interest in local politics.

"Councillor Prodding," replied the Countess.

"Mm, Prodding... Prodding, that name rings a bell. Where have I heard that before?"

Celestia May chipped in. "He's the chairman of the Cress Society," she said. "He despises you."

"There's no way Prodding will take a bribe," said Hatcher.

"In that case," supposed Hardy, smacking his hands together, "we will have to kill him."

"Lord and Lady Ingleby-Barwick!" O'Donnell

announced from the hallway, and as Angus blustered his way into the Great Sitting Room, O'Donnell gently closed the door behind him.

"What's all this about a duel?" he asked.

"Oh, they won't go through with it," said Hogg-Marchmont, "it's just a bit of banter."

"Duel?" sniffed the Countess.

Nothing in this house got past Celestia May. "Yes, haven't you heard, Mother? O'Donnell found one of Father's friends in bed with Mrs. Frapp, and now he's going to shoot him."

"I absolutely forbid it," said Isabella. "I'm not having a servant shooting one of my husband's friends. Which friend is it, anyway?"

"It's Melton Thornaby," revealed Celestia May.

"That odious monster?" screamed the Countess. "Oh, he's welcome to kill him. Can Thornaby shoot?"

"Of course he can't shoot," said Hardy.

"Good," replied Isabella.

"Can O'Donnell shoot?" asked Hatcher.

"He was in the army for three years," said Hardy.

"Where's Thornaby now?" asked the Countess.

"Last seen hiding in the folly," replied Hardy. "The duel's set for tomorrow afternoon at three."

"I'll bring a picnic," said Ingleby-Barwick, and he leapt onto the sofa, excitedly clapping his hands. "How romantic. No one's ever offered to fight a duel for me."

So that he might avoid O'Donnell, Thornaby came into the Great Sitting Room via the French windows. He sat down sheepishly on the Chesterfield next to the First Earl's third favourite suit of armour. He'd worn this armour around the time that Hogg Hall declared war on France. The war did not last very long and concluded with the Great Battle of the Lake in 1798. The First Earl lined up his forces on the south side of the Sluice Gates, his army consisting of a hundred or so servants and peasants armed to the teeth with farm implements and pointed sticks. On the north side stood twenty-three thousand elite French troops, muskets loaded, bayonets fixed, their tunics bright blue against the treeline. The battle lasted for a surprisingly protracted twelve seconds, and while the First Earl was surrendering to the French, he became trapped in his armour and rather embarrassingly had to be cut out of it with a device resembling a tin opener.

Hatcher and Lady Labia pointed their noses at the ceiling and flounced out of the Great Sitting Room, closely followed by the Countess, who looked at Melton Thornaby as if she'd like to slow roast him on a spit.

"Well come on," said Ingleby-Barwick, "tell us all the gory details."

"I don't remember anything!" cried Thornaby. "She was just there when I woke up."

"I'm sure O'Donnell is not actually going to kill you," reassured Hardy, "he's a trained marksman. He'll probably just teach you a lesson by shooting off one of your ears."

"But I need both of my ears," sobbed Melton. "Can't you have a word with him? He's your servant."

"O'Donnell is his own man," replied the Sixth Earl. "If he requires satisfaction, I cannot, as a gentleman, intervene."

"Hardy," snapped Melton, "you've never behaved like a gentleman in the past, so why the fuck should you start behaving like one now? Just tell him that if he kills me, you'll fire him."

"I'm sorry, Thornaby," said Hogg-Marchmont, "I can't do that. It's a question of honour. O'Donnell has made up his mind. You must face him on the duelling ground."

When Mrs. Frapp heard that O'Donnell was prepared to die for her honour, she was moved to tears, and for a while she actually forgot that Melton Thornaby was innocent of any wrongdoing. Nelly felt she had three options. She could tell O'Donnell the truth; she could let the duel go ahead and hope that neither man managed to shoot the other; or she could fall on her sword.

For just such an occasion, Nelly kept an 1897 British infantry sword. The weapon had a heavily etched, thirty-inch blade, a razor-sharp spear point, and it had been carried by the Third Earl during the Boer War. Mrs. Frapp had fallen on this sword three times before. The first time was in 1966, following an unpleasant experience in the Great Sitting Room with Lord Heathcote of Lanarkshire. The second time was in 1975 when the cheese soufflé she served to the Archbishop of Canterbury had collapsed, causing huge embarrassment to the Fifth Earl and his wife. On the third occasion, during the 1980s, Mrs. Frapp had simply fallen on the sword by accident. All three times, the doctors at Muddleton Cottage Hospital A&E had dutifully stitched and bandaged Nelly's wounds and sent her back to Hogg Hall in a taxi.

After much thought and soul searching, Nelly decided that falling on her sword was not the best option. In any case, there was nothing she liked better than a good duel, and she didn't really like Melton Thornaby very much.

Men prepare to meet their maker in many ways, and Melton's way was firstly to open a bottle of 2007 Chablis Vaudesir. As he enjoyed the wine's engaging nose of iodine, salt and intense seashore aromas, he suddenly realised that there was a very real chance that this would be his last full day on earth. His next thought was that at twenty-five stone, he was approximately three times the width of O'Donnell, presenting the Irishman a considerably larger target than he himself would have to aim at.

Melton's life began to flash before him. During his time with the Muddleton Wine Society, he had tasted an average of around four thousand wines annually – all of which he had swallowed, and not one drop of which had ended up in a spit bucket. The concentration of fruit, tannins, alcohol and acid had been of little interest to him, and he had always been far more concerned about quantity than quality. In Melton's world, wine tastings were for getting stinking drunk. Did this make him a bad person? Well, yes, of course it did.

Melton had once told a reporter from the Italian magazine *Al Volante* that 'fine wine is like a woman's genitalia: succulent, mysterious and only unavailable to those who can afford it'. Why he gave an Italian car magazine a quote about wine is a mystery to this day, but this enigmatic and deeply sexist little simile somehow managed to propel him to minor fame as a wine writer.

Melton meticulously updated his wine blog twice a year and spent the rest of the time attempting to blag his way into tastings, or trying to empty the contents of the Hogg-Marchmont wine cellar.

But during his long and disagreeable life, Melton had unearthed more than one way of irreparably damaging his health. In 2008, in collaboration with a young filmmaker called James Cudd, Melton had produced, presented and appeared in a 240-minute documentary called *No Smoke Without Cigars*. He had travelled across Cuba, interviewing various well-known personalities in the region, all of whom had varying degrees of self-inflicted lung disease. The film premiered at the Havana Film Festival in December 2009, but nobody could see it because there was too much cigar smoke in the cinema. During this project, Melton smoked around 1,500 cigars, severely damaging one of his lungs and completely destroying the other.

Still residing in the Queen of Scots Bedroom, Melton continued drinking late into the night, then he fell into a deep sleep, which might have been his last.

O'Donnell, meanwhile, was preparing for the following day's duel in a far more focused way. The servant lay fully clothed on his bed, listening to the quiet drone of the bees and slowly clenching and unclenching his fists. This would not be the first time that Quinn had been called upon to kill an Englishman.

The 'three years' military service' that appeared on his CV failed to mention that this was time spent in the Irish Republican Army. O'Donnell had seen some bad things that it was good not to talk about. He'd also seen some good things that it was bad not to talk about.

O'Donnell clenched and unclenched his fists for a further ten minutes, and then he drifted off to sleep. There was serious business to be done next day.

Chapter Eight

As the agreed time approached, family, servants and guests gathered at the clearing in the woods that was the appointed site for duelling with pistols. Steady, incessant drizzle had started around dawn and carried on late into the morning. Around midday, Melton Thornaby suggested that the duel might be 'rained off'.

"This isn't a cricket match at Lords," Hogg-Marchmont replied, and he continued to carefully clean the barrels of the family flintlocks.

At 2.55pm, Thornaby and O'Donnell stood next to each other in the clearing in the woods, shivering in the cold and damp. Melton had chosen Ingleby-Barwick, appropriately dressed in a 'Scottish Widows' hooded gown, to be his second. O'Donnell had selected Viscount Hatcher. The seconds both held loaded pistols, ready to hand them to the two combatants when the fateful moment arrived.

Thornaby and the African were both so drunk they could hardly see, and surprisingly O'Donnell's breath too, smelt a little of Irish whiskey.

Sharing a large golfing umbrella, Celestia May stood watching with her sister-in-law Lady Labia Antoinette – the baby looked after, meanwhile, by Nanny Alice, who seemed very confused about what exactly was going to happen. The child slept soundly in his pram, its canopy raised to protect him from the elements. Countess Isabella was notable by her absence. She'd flatly refused to attend the proceedings and was instead in London, shopping for cushions at John Lewis.

Viewing the proceedings from behind a nearby blasted oak was Nelly Frapp, who had driven herself down to the lake in her second-hand mobility scooter, the wheels of which were now thickly caked in mud.

Duels are traditionally fought not to kill one's opponent, but to gain satisfaction by demonstrating a willingness to risk one's life for one's honour. O'Donnell felt safe in the knowledge that he was fighting for the honour of his fellow servant Mrs. Frapp, and Melton was now so hammered, he couldn't remember why the fuck he was there at all.

Duelling is exclusively reserved for members of the nobility, and it is considered extremely poor taste for such combat to involve a servant. Had Hardy thought of that loophole earlier, he might have been able to extract Melton from this horror show on a technicality. But now it was too late. It was one minute to three.

"This duel shall be carried out according to the Hogg Hall code of 1791," announced the Sixth Earl, "which sets out dignified duelling behaviour for the Hogg-Marchmont family."

He went on, "No shooting or firing in the air is admissible. Duellists may not use dummy bullets or declare ahead of time that they will fire their weapons into the air or at non-vital areas of their opponent's body."

Melton hiccupped, giggled and whispered in his second's ear, "Which part of my body would you say was non-vital?" he asked.

"Your brain," replied Ingleby-Barwick, and he offered Thornaby a final swig from his hip flask. Thornaby lit a cigar and puffed on it until it made him wheeze and cough like an invalid. If he was going to die in a minute's time, he might as well indulge himself.

"No smoking," yelled Hogg-Marchmont, and he snatched the Havana from Melton's mouth, flicked off the ash with his fingernail and popped it into his top pocket for later.

"There shall be at least ten yards' distance between the combatants," instructed Hogg-Marchmont, "then the seconds shall present pistols to the principals. The weapons must not be cocked before delivery."

Hatcher led O'Donnell out into the centre of the duelling ground, and he handed him one of the flintlock pistols. Hardy paced out ten yards from O'Donnell and drew a line in the mud with his heel. His arm around his friend, Ingleby-Barwick helped Melton to wade through the mud of the clearing and stand behind the ten-yard line. He steadied him as best he could, but Melton swayed back and forth alarmingly and began to sing, 'You Make Me Feel So Young'. He was quickly silenced as Hogg-Marchmont called out an instruction to his second.

"Angus, give him the pistol," he said.

"Oh my God," murmured Celestia May, and everyone suddenly realised that this was really going to happen.

"Are they actually going to shoot at each other?" asked Nanny Alice.

"Welcome to Hogg Hall," said Lady Labia.

Nanny Alice was having something of a baptism of fire with the Hogg-Marchmont family. She'd been screamed at, sicked upon and shat upon, and that was only when the baby wasn't in the room. She'd already threatened to resign from her position twice but had been told by Lady Labia that she had to serve out her full one-month notice period or she would not be paid for the work she'd done already. There were three things in the world that Nanny Alice hated. Lady Labia Antoinette, the film *The Sound of Music* and babies.

Angus handed the gun to Melton, and his hand began to shake. Hogg-Marchmont made a penultimate announcement. "The combatants are to present and shoot together, at the agreed signal. First, I shall ask you to cock your pistols, and then I shall say three, two, one, fire."

The weather turned abruptly from light rain to a heavy downpour. Melton Thornaby felt his waterproof pants fill up with a malodorous mixture of rain, urine and faecal matter.

"Each combatant shall fire one shot," explained Hardy, "and if neither is hit, but the challenger is satisfied, the duel shall be declared over."

Thornaby began to sing Sinatra again. This time it was 'Come Fly With Me'.

"Be quiet, Thornaby!" shouted Hogg-Marchmont. "It's time."

Nelly Frapp decided that this had gone on long enough. She called out for them to stop, but the storm was now far too loud for her frail voice to carry. She tried to move her mobility scooter closer to the clearing, but it stuck fast in the mud.

"Gentlemen, cock your pistols!" shouted Hardy.

With a single click, O'Donnell cocked his pistol and raised it to point at his opponent. Thornaby fumbled and bungled about with the mechanism of his weapon. He had never cocked a pistol before. After thirty seconds of hopelessly buggering around, Hardy ran out and cocked it for him, before dashing back to his referee's position. Melton raised his pistol and pointed it at O'Donnell.

"Three…" said Hardy, "two…"

"Wait, wait!" shouted Melton. "Which one's the trigger again?"

Hardy splashed out though the puddles again and showed Thornaby where the trigger was. His compatriot almost pulled it by mistake, but Hardy steadied his hand. The Sixth Earl waded back to his position.

"Can you go back to three again?" asked Melton.

O'Donnell looked at Hogg-Marchmont and sighed.

"Three…" called Hardy, his tiny ears twitching, "two…"

Melton's hand trembled, and his entire body leaned over like the Tower of Pisa. He wiped a raindrop away from his eyelid. O'Donnell's hand was steady as a rock, as he tried to remember whether he was supposed to shoot after 'one' or 'fire'. Then two entirely unscheduled things happened. First, there was a deafening growl, like that of a wild animal, from the trees behind where Celestia May and Lady Labia were standing.

"What the fuck was that?" asked Hardy.

Second, there was the sound of a fast-approaching

police siren, and the gloomy day was straightaway illuminated by a flashing blue light.

"Run for it!" yelled Hardy, and everyone beat a hasty retreat and disappeared behind the trees. By the time the police car had wheel-spun and skidded its way across the north lawn, the duelling ground was deserted. Muddleton Constabulary were well used to responding to reports of peculiar rites and rituals at Hogg Hall. After half-heartedly shining their torches around in the woods for a couple of minutes, PC Hardmeat and WPC Foreman-Grill jumped back into their squad car and headed back into town.

"Who grassed us up?" said Thornaby, and then he toppled forwards and his huge body landed face down with a clump. The entire company, with the exception of Nelly Frapp, had by now arrived at the Fisting Room in the Great Folly, and they were drying themselves off. Hogg-Marchmont attempted to take the cocked and loaded pistol from Melton's hand, but it discharged with a surprisingly loud crack, a piece of lead shot embedding itself between the eyes of an oil painting of the Third Earl. Hardy turned to O'Donnell, and he indicated Melton snoring resonantly on the floor.

"Do you still want to shoot him?" he asked.

"Yes," replied O'Donnell, "but I won't," and he handed his pistol back to Hardy.

"We shall never speak of this again!" declared the Sixth Earl. All at once, there was an ear-splitting scream.

"Now what?" sighed Hardy.

"The baby! Where's the baby?" howled Lady Labia Antoinette.

"He's in the pram!" said Nanny Alice.

"No, he isn't!" insisted Lady Labia. "He's gone!"

Nanny Alice had swiftly wheeled the pram into the Great Folly, immediately following the arrival of the police. Before leaving the clearing, she'd had no reason to check to see if the baby was still sleeping safely inside.

"My baby! My baby!" shrieked Lady Labia.

"He was there, I swear," sobbed Nanny Alice.

The phone rang at Muddleton Constabulary, and it was answered by the duty officer Sergeant Foot. After jotting down a few details, he reassured the caller. "OK, we'll send a car right away," he said.

"Anyone in the vicinity of Hogg Hall?" Foot barked into the radio.

The voice of PC Hardmeat crackled back from the other end. "Seriously?" he said.

That evening, the police were not very helpful at all. Hogg Hall was now little more than a joke to the boys and girls in blue.

"Are you absolutely sure you had a baby?" PC Hardmeat asked Lady Labia in the Great Sitting Room.

"Of course we're sure," Hatcher insisted.

"Do you have a birth certificate?" asked WPC Foreman-Grill.

When the police suggested that the couple should simply 'check in the pram again', Hatcher flew into a rage and demanded that the officers examine the baby buggy themselves. PC Hardmeat lifted up the infant's blanket and double-checked underneath it. WPC Foreman-Grill crouched down and surveyed the underside of the pram. "Nope," she said, "there's definitely no baby here."

Celestia May stepped out of the shadows, making

everyone jump. She had an annoying habit of doing that. "It was the Beast," she whispered. "I heard it. Everyone heard it."

"Beast?" repeated Nanny Alice.

"But the child is safe," said Celestia May.

"How do you know?" asked Lady Labia.

"I can feel it," the girl replied. It was the worst thing she could possibly have said. The police left within minutes, and WPC Foreman-Grill simply scribbled in her notebook, *Child safe*.

*

Next morning, Lady Labia was much too upset to join the others for breakfast. Her husband Viscount Hatcher, however, sat eating toast soldiers, dipped into a soft-boiled egg for him by O'Donnell. The servant had been doing this for Hatcher since he was three years old, and at this time of family crisis, there was no reason to stop. The rest of the family were also in the Great Dining Room, but the mood was understandably downbeat.

Modelling the slender black dress worn by Holly Golightly in *Breakfast at Tiffany's*, Ingleby-Barwick sat with Melton Thornaby at the table. The pair sat nursing their hangovers by drinking Americano laced with Moldovan vodka, and Melton had little or no memory of the previous couple of day's events, which was probably just as well. O'Donnell finished feeding eggy soldiers to Hatcher, and the Viscount could hold back no longer. "We must go and search the woods!" he demanded.

"You have to say," pointed out the Countess, "that

Celestia May is usually pretty good when it comes to this sort of thing. She knew exactly where that kitten had got to last Christmas."

This was true. It had taken Celestia May just ten minutes to locate the kitten in the Great Tithe Barn, or at least what was left of it, after it had been taken from its basket and ripped to shreds by the resident barn owl.

"The baby is safe," Celestia May said again. "The Beast shall take care of it and raise it as though it were her own."

"But I don't want my son to be brought up in the woods by a wild creature!" screamed Hatcher.

"Why on earth not?" asked Thornaby.

Hogg-Marchmont put a halt to the discussion. "Hatcher is right," he said. "We must all go and search for baby Keith, and we must do it now!"

"Do I have time for one more coffee?" asked Thornaby.

*

O'Donnell returned to his room and changed into a pair of stout boots, ready for the search in the woods. There was more noise than usual coming from the beehive under his bed. Anthogrid, Arvid and Egil had not returned from that morning's forage in the south meadow, and the house bees were humming with concern.

"Should we send a search party?" asked one of the drones.

"It's too early for that," replied a nurse bee. "I'm sure they'll be home soon."

A huge crab spider had set his trap well. He'd skilfully spun the fine threads of his web between two large sunflowers, and Anthogrid, attracted by the bright yellow petals, had flown straight into the web and become stuck fast.

"Oh fuckity fuck," said the tiny bee.

The crab spider was now slowly lowering itself towards him, its razor-sharp jaws chomping hungrily. Arvid and Egil had tried to rescue Anthogrid, but now they too were stuck fast in the fine spiral of silk. The spider studied all three captured insects and opted to approach Arvid first, as he looked the tastiest. He wrapped his legs around the bee's plump body and wasted no time in biting off his head and devouring it.

"Is this a good time to talk about Earth, Wind & Fire?" asked Anthogrid.

Egil laughed. "Probably not," he said.

A few minutes later, the crab spider grew bored with munching on Arvid's dry carcass, and he crawled his way towards Egil.

"It's been a privilege flying with you, kid," said the seasoned old bee, and he saluted Anthogrid with his only free foreleg. Moments later, he was dead. But fate had a lot more in store for Anthogrid. It was not his destiny to die dangling from a crab spider's web in the south meadow. As Egil's limp body separated from his head, it dropped a few centimetres and its weight tore open the tiniest of gaps in the web. Anthogrid saw his chance, and while the spider was busy digesting the thorax of his mentor, he wriggled free and took flight. His wings were still covered with acrid, gluey solvent from the spider's web, but he soon built up some momentum and managed to set an unsteady northwards course for Hogg Hall.

*

Lady Celestia May was having one of her mystical days. It began in the early hours of the morning with a crystal-clear vision of a demonic beast tenderly suckling a human child. This reverie calmed the girl, and she rose at 5.30am and walked down to the wooden swing seat next to the observatory. It was an old hardwood two-seater, with a comfortable bench and a weathered canopy. Celestia May swung lazily to and fro, kicking out her bare legs and remembering how she had loved to sit in this place with her father when she was little more than a toddler.

"Caw, caw!" said a crow, and its coarse sound echoed back from the curved walls of the Great Folly and whispered, "Caw, caw," again in the middle distance.

As she quite often did when it was a waxing moon, Celestia May had dreamed that night of rebirth, renewal and transmigration of the spirit. As a watery sun rose above the lake, she became suddenly aware that she was the reincarnation of a girl called Mary Isobel Catherine Bernadette O'Brien. Having no idea who that person was, she googled it on her phone. There was very slow mobile broadband that morning, but she eventually came up with a result. It seemed that Celestia May was the reincarnation of Dusty Springfield.

Mary Isobel Catherine Bernadette O'Brien, known professionally as Dusty, had died on 2 March 1999, just one day before Celestia May had been born at Hogg Hall. Dusty was a pop singer whose career extended from the late 1950s to the 1990s, and at her peak, she was one of the most successful English female performers of all time, with six top-twenty singles in America and sixteen in the UK. After being in various groups, her solo career took off in 1963 with a song called, 'I Only Want To Be With You'.

As soon as she got back to her room, Celestia May printed off a picture of the singer and pinned it on the wall next to her dressing mirror. Dusty's peroxide blonde hair and heavy, dark eye make-up fascinated the girl, and it wasn't long before she had downloaded every song that Dusty ever recorded. 'I Just Don't Know What To Do With Myself' (1964), 'You Don't Have To Say You Love Me' (1966). Celestia May's favourite by far was 'Son of a Preacher Man' (1968). She printed off the lyrics and watched Dusty singing it on YouTube over and over again. It was only three hours since Celestia May had sensed that she was the reincarnation of Dusty Springfield, and now this woman's life engulfed her; it defined her and it completed her. She would never be the same again.

To be fair, exactly the same thing had happened when, two weeks earlier, she had announced that she was the reincarnation of Anne Boleyn, and the previous month she'd been the reincarnation of Grace Kelly, Aretha Franklin and George Washington. Some of the people Celestia May claimed to be the reincarnation of were not even dead yet, but she'd had all their faces indelibly tattooed on various parts of her body.

*

The pig gargoyles looked down benevolently as everyone from Hogg Hall made their way purposefully towards the woods to search for baby Keith. They were joined by a handful of locals from the Pig & Pencil Case, plus the Muddleton Morris Men and a few of the monks from Ghastbury Abbey. Melton Thornaby was holding one of those spikes you use to pick up litter, and he was carrying a black bin bag. O'Donnell had a rifle over his shoulder in case he should come face to face with the Beast. Hardy's mistress, Lady Prunella Box-Girder, had also decided that it would be good to be seen at a baby hunt, and she had agonised long and hard about the appropriate hat to wear. She had finally settled on a bright pink Failsworth Lily Fascinator, which she wore perched on the side of her head like a puffin clinging to a rock face. This came with matching pink suedette shoes and a fuchsia Dolce & Gabbana shoulder bag, with a gold clasp.

Lady Prunella found it increasingly difficult to keep her balance in her high heels as the search party fanned out into a long line and began poking at the dense undergrowth in front of them.

"Don't worry, I'm sure the baby is fine," Nanny Alice whispered to Lady Labia Antoinette, who had been strongly advised not to join the search but insisted on coming anyway.

Lady Labia was pumped with so much prescription medicine and antidepressants, she probably could not feel her feet, but she still managed to hiss an unpleasant reply in the direction of the nanny. "No thanks to you," she said.

"Of course, you know that this is your fault," the Countess told her husband.

"How is this my fault?" replied Hardy in his usual innocent and slightly hurt tone. He rearranged his jockey shorts uncomfortably and tried to change the subject.

"D'you know," he confided quietly, "I've got a nasty feeling that all this stress is about to bring on another episode of my haemorrhoids."

Isabella ignored this tactic. "If you hadn't let that ridiculous duel go ahead," she said, "Lady Labia and the baby wouldn't have been at the lake in the first place."

"Who takes a baby to a duel?" Hardy replied, and for just a moment, his wife could not help but agree with him. Hatcher shuffled along next to Lord and Lady Ingleby-Barwick, and without warning, there was a thunderous growl from deep inside the woods. It sounded like something tearing something else to shreds. Hatcher stopped in his tracks, and Angus tried to lighten the mood.

"This reminds me of when you and I and your father used to go grouse shooting," he said. "Do you remember those days?"

Hatcher did not reply. He just stared at Ingleby-Barwick like a sparrow hawk stares at a sparrow. Then he set off again, mopping sweat from his brow and muttering under his breath.

*

Like trout fishing, grouse shooting at Hogg Hall was an unconventional and singular pursuit. Every August, on the 'Glorious Twelfth', Hardy would take his son down to Hogg Hall's famous grouse moors, and Mr. O'Donnell, Mrs. Frapp and a footman called Mr. Cedwyn would act as 'beaters', driving the grouse towards the Hogg-Marchmonts by waving flags, thrashing the undergrowth with sticks and singing 'Jerusalem' in resounding three-part harmony. For health and safety reasons, and for the purpose of etiquette, there was a strict code of conduct governing behaviour on the grouse moors. This code of conduct was of course comprehensively ignored by Hardy Hogg-Marchmont, and as a result, the sport was considerably more exhilarating.

In most shooting parties, the hunters use twelve-bore, lightweight shotguns and stand in a 'hide', which is screened by a turf wall and sunk into the ground to minimise their profile. The problem with this method is that a flock of scattering grouse fly at over 80mph and can be inordinately tricky to hit.

At Hogg Hall, the shooting party would assemble in the Fourth Earl's Second World War concrete bunker, and they would dispatch the grouse using Russian automatic assault rifles. Set on fully automatic, these weapons could fire around six hundred rounds per minute, and not a single grouse had ever been known to survive the exercise. It was on one occasion like this, that a nine-year-old Viscount Hatcher, unbeknown to either himself or his father, accidentally shot Mr. Cedwyn in the knee. Not wishing to alert either the family or the authorities, O'Donnell humanely finished the Welshman off with a single shot to the head, and he asked the gamekeeper to dispose of his body during the next round of heather burning on the moorland. Sad to report, the red grouse is now entirely extinct within a two-hundred-mile radius of Hogg Hall.

Countess Isabella had never searched the woods for a missing baby before, but since accidentally falling in love with Hardy and marrying into the Hogg-Marchmont family, her life had been abundant with a catalogue of burdensome and arduous incidents.

She had been brought up to expect so much more. Her childhood had been a comfortable and serene one. Her father, Humphrey Tapp-Fawcett, had made his fortune by working the Muddleton Fish Mines, which had been rich in salmon in the 1960s.

It's probably worth mentioning that fish mines are not a common occurrence, it usually being possible to fish for salmon on the surface. However, the unusual geographical features of the area surrounding Muddleton Point, meant that the river flowed deep underground in some areas, making it only possible to reach the salmon by sinking a broad mineshaft into the rock. Fish mining is extremely dangerous, and many miners drowned during excavations. But the industry made Isabella's father an extremely rich man. Unfortunately, he disowned Isabella when she married Hogg-Marchmont, and her life was never the same again. Even on their romantic honeymoon in Malta, Hardy had got drunk and joined a very dodgy backstreet poker game in Valetta. As a direct result, they had both fallen into the hands of a notorious group of Italian kidnappers, who had imprisoned them on a private yacht in Golden Bay. As it turned out, the yacht was far better accommodation than the apartment they'd been staying in, and the Countess and Hardy became firm friends with the gang members, as soon as it was discovered that the Hogg-Marchmont family were penniless and unable to pay any ransom money.

One of the gang, an ex-Mafia boss called Alessandro Alessandro, eventually became a godparent to Celestia May and to this day their daughter was the only girl in Muddleton with a godfather who was a Godfather. It had proved extremely useful on several occasions to have connections in the Cosa Nostra.

Isabella had stood by her husband through law suits, court cases, death threats, betting scandals, property scams and worse. Despite this, her formula for a moderately passable marriage remained unchanged and was based on the simple premise that a wife should love her husband, but not too much.

When the Sixth Earl screwed up, as he so frequently did, she would always leave him forever, then return a couple of days later to find him miraculously redeemed and restored. She called it 'pressing Hardy's reset button'. She also took care to sleep with him at least once a year, whether he requested it or not.

*

The hunt for baby Keith carried on late into the evening, the search made ever more dangerous as darkness fell, by the treacherous peat bogs that were dotted throughout the woods. As mist drifted above the brushwood, and the owls began their twilight conversations, Hogg-Marchmont caught up with Melton Thornaby in the furthest and murkiest corner of the forest.

"Any news?" Hardy asked his friend.

"Nothing," replied Thornaby.

"This may not be the time," said Melton, "but there is something I'd like to do for you."

"What's that?" asked Hardy.

"I want you to let me use my showbiz contacts to put on a big fundraising event for Hogg Hall."

"Fundraiser?" asked Hogg-Marchmont.

"Maybe some kind of celebrity wine tasting," explained Thornaby. "You know the kind of thing, a few B-listers, some skinny models in swimsuits and a bunch of pissed journalists. If you can get the press on your side, you might be able to save this old place yet."

Hardy knew that this was one of the worst ideas he'd ever heard, but he did not have the heart to throw it back in his friend's face, and he found himself agreeing to it. What could possibly go wrong?

Chapter Nine

The Muddleton Morris Men picked their way through the undergrowth at the far end of the north woods. They'd been searching for the baby now since mid-morning and were determined to be the ones to find Master Keith safe and well. The six men were no strangers to search and rescue. They were the only Morris dancing team in England to double up as a lifeboat crew and had bravely manned the Muddleton Lifeboat for over twenty years, saving dozens of lives while still proudly wearing their sashes, waistcoats and wooden clogs.

In 2002, the Morris Men became national celebrities when they bravely rescued three schoolchildren trapped underground in the old abandoned fish mines. As a result, they were asked to record a Christmas charity single and reached number six in the UK charts with their a cappella cover version of 'We'll Lift You Up'. The Morris Men also played six-a-side football, and two thirds of them won bronze at the 1998 Winter Olympics as a four-man bobsleigh team.

As the Morris Men stumbled and bumbled their way through the woods, they suddenly heard an almighty, blood-curdling growl, and it stopped them dead in their tracks. The sound was quickly followed by heavy panting, as though something was running, exhausted, through the bracken.

"That's either the Beast or Melton Thornaby out for a jog," said Ben Dunn. But no one laughed.

The Morris Men stopped for liquid refreshment by the Great Henry Oak, a huge tree that was known to be over eight hundred years old.

The tree weighed an estimated twenty-five tons, had a girth of forty feet and a canopy of over a hundred feet. It was almost entirely hollow at the base, and legend told that the young Henry III had hidden inside the oak in order to evade capture by Rebel Barons. American tourists of course lapped this up, but the Sixth Earl was only nine years old when he worked out that when Henry III was alive, the tree was only the size of a sapling and was barely large enough to conceal a squirrel. This was a tried and tested subterfuge known as the Sherwood Deception, having been invented by the tourist board in Nottingham to drive footfall to a large tree in Sherwood Forest.

According to local folklore, the tree was Robin Hood's shelter and was where he and about twenty of his merry men slept. When Robin Hood was alive, if indeed he ever was, the tree would have been only two feet tall, but despite this inconsistency, it was voted England's Tree of the Year in 2014, receiving eighteen per cent of the votes.

"I am not putting ointment on your husband's arse!" protested Nanny Alice.

"I don't see why not," reasoned Countess Isabella. "You put ointment on the baby's arse."

"It's my job to put ointment on the baby's arse!" said Nanny Alice. "Why can't you do it? You're his wife."

"We're not having sexual relations at the moment," revealed the Countess.

"How is applying haemorrhoid cream sexual relations?" asked Nanny Alice.

"You're the only member of staff available," explained Isabella, "I've asked Mrs. Frapp and she refused, even though she's been tending to Hardy's anus one way or another since he was a week old. She says she doesn't have a steady enough hand anymore."

"Well, what about Mr. O'Donnell?" asked the nanny.

"He is too senior," sniffed the Countess. "If you won't do it, I will have to ask you to look for another situation."

"This is the twenty-first century," screamed Nanny Alice, "you can't sack me for refusing to put ointment on a man's arse!"

"Oh yes I can!" insisted Isabella. "In any case, I seem to remember that you have also managed to lose my grandson."

Nanny Alice stormed out of the room and slammed the door behind her. Alice was no Mary Poppins, and it wasn't the first time she'd mislaid a baby. She was losing them all the time, and not a single one of her glowing references was genuine. She'd once lost Princess Birgitta of Denmark in Tesco's car park, and it had taken her three days to find Crown Prince Masako of Japan, after she left his baby seat in the back of a minicab in Tottenham Court Road. Alice had carelessly mislaid the heirs of barons, dukes, tsars and, on one occasion, the twin sons of a sultan. Most of the infants had turned up safe and sound, but it had sometimes been necessary to do a midnight flit, before her employers checked their nurseries first thing in the morning.

Hardy was in the Great Sitting Room, but there wasn't any sitting going on. He was lying face down on the right-hand facing Edwardian chaise longue, and Ingleby-Barwick, in a shimmering gold tracksuit, was medicating him by syphoning Hennessy Cognac into his mouth, by means of a long plastic tube. It was at times like this that one found out who one's true friends were. Meanwhile, Melton Thornaby sat at a Norwegian pine side table and talked loudly on his phone.

"What do you mean, she can't do the wine tasting?" he boomed. "Fiona Bruce owes me a huge favour. If it wasn't for me, she'd have got five years for sneaking that nineteenth-century carriage clock out of Hogg Hall. We should never have had the *Antiques Road Show* here, those thieving BBC bastards!"

He slammed down the phone. "Right, I've got Esther Rantzen, Angela Rippon and Paul Daniels," he told the recumbent Hogg-Marchmont.

"Aren't they all dead?" asked the Sixth Earl.

"At least one of them's dead," pointed out Ingleby-Barwick.

"Which one?" asked Hardy.

"I'm not sure," said Angus.

"Can't you get any modern-day celebrities?" ranted Hogg-Marchmont. "I thought you had connections in showbusiness."

"I'm doing my best," sighed Melton. "I have a heavy pencil on Jon Tickle."

"Who the fuck is Jon Tickle?" screamed Hardy.

"He was in *Big Brother* in 2003," said Thornaby.

"This is going to be a fucking disaster," said Hogg-Marchmont.

"But there is good news," gushed Melton, "I've got a thousand bottles of wine being donated."

"Well at least that's something," said Hardy. "Which vineyard is donating it?"

"Lidl," replied Melton.

Hogg-Marchmont howled, and no one was quite sure if this outburst was caused by what Thornaby had just said, or by the Sixth Earl's increasingly troublesome arsehole.

Melton Thornaby's celebrity connections were sparse to say the least, but he was immensely fond of bigging himself up in company. At the Licensed Victuallers Exhibition at Earls Court in 1972, he'd once accidentally spilt wine over Felicity Kendal, and the resulting social intercourse had led to the pair briefly renting a house together in the Dordogne, at which they endlessly played Demis Roussos records and entertained a galaxy of stars including Joanna Lumley, Jimmy Tarbuck and Keith Harris and Orville.

More recently, Thornaby was briefly engaged to the newsreader Moira Stuart but had to break off the relationship when he accidentally set fire to her flat, resulting in the loss of her priceless collection of pizza wheels and the death of two poodles called Florence and The Machine.

"The servants have gone on strike," the Countess told Hardy as he waited for his lunch while lying flat on his stomach on the dining table.

"Strike?" he shouted. "Why would they want to go on strike?"

"Because I sacked Nanny Alice," she said.

"Is this to do with my haemorrhoids?" Hardy sighed, although he already knew that the answer was yes.

"I'll give it a few hours, reinstate the nanny, and then everything will be back to normal," the Countess told her husband.

"A few hours?" screamed Melton Thornaby, who had invited himself to lunch. "How on earth are we going to survive with no servants for a few hours?"

Hardy rang the little bell on the dining table.

"It's no good ringing that," said the Countess, "O'Donnell is upstairs in bed."

"Well, what are we going to eat?" screeched Hardy.

"I have absolutely no idea," replied the Countess. "I suppose I could try making some toast, but I can't guarantee I'll be able to work the toaster."

Melton clapped his hands. "Oh well, chin up," he said. "Who's for a liquid lunch? I'll pop down to the wine cellar and get a couple of bottles."

"O'Donnell has the keys to the wine cellar," said Hogg-Marchmont grimly, and Melton turned very pale indeed.

Meanwhile, Lady Labia was having gruesome

nightmares – the most recent and vivid one involving Viscount Hatcher trying to attach a nappy to the baby by means of a staple gun. In the dream, Lady Labia had somehow managed to cover herself, and most of the interior of Hogg Hall, in her son's bright yellow excrement, and her husband was vomiting violently.

"We must feed it," she was screaming in the dream. "What does it eat? What does the baby eat?"

In the absence of Nanny Alice, similar scenes would probably have been occurring for real that very morning, had the baby been safe and well at Hogg Hall. Lady Labia had never changed a nappy in her life, and she had once believed that newborn babies ate Kellogg's Frosties and Marmite sandwiches.

She herself had been brought up by a team of six wet nurses, who took it in turns to breastfeed her and, at the end of each day, formed themselves into a Baroque choir, to send her to sleep by singing the Mass in B minor by Johann Sebastian Bach.

To say she was spoilt was an understatement. Having been born on 14 July, Lady Labia was fourteen years old before she realised that the French national holiday was not to celebrate her birthday.

*

Viscount Hatcher had already given up hope on baby Keith and was convinced that his son would never return alive from the woods. People deal with grief in different ways, and that morning Hatcher had driven into Muddleton town centre and bought a present for his wife.

"What's this?" Lady Labia asked, when Hatcher presented it to her in a gift box.

"It's a puppy," replied her husband.

"Yes, I know it is a puppy," she said, "but what is it doing here?"

"I thought it would cheer you up," Hatcher told his wife. "You know, what with the baby disappearing and everything."

The tiny dog was clearly in distress and was whimpering. It was only a few days old and had been taken from its mother way too soon. At a time of anguish for the family, Hatcher had successfully managed to bring even more distress into Hogg Hall, by making a small animal unhappy. It was his destiny to be a dick all of his life, and he was never going to take a day off.

"I don't want it," snapped Lady Labia.

"Well, what am I supposed to do with it?" asked Hatcher.

"I don't know," said his wife. "Drown it?"

Hatcher took hold of the dog and it promptly pissed on his shirt. Holding it at arm's length, he removed the animal from his wife's sight and headed towards the Great Bathroom on the first floor. As Hatcher filled the bath with cold water, the puppy looked at him adoringly, and it wagged its tail. It was an English cocker spaniel with big brown eyes and long, brown curly ears. As he lifted the dog into the water, it yelped loudly, and Celestia May, who happened to be passing, poked her head around the door.

"What are you doing?" she asked her brother.

"I'm drowning a puppy," he said.

"That's not how you drown a puppy," she replied. "Give it to me."

Celestia May took hold of the dog, and it yelped again as the cold water splashed over its dangling rear paws.

At that moment, Countess Isabella happened to be winding the Burlington grandfather clock, a job which was usually O'Donnell's. When she heard the sound of a dog yapping at the far end of the corridor, she peered into the Great Bathroom.

"What are you doing?" she asked her son and daughter.

"We're drowning a puppy," they replied.

Countess Isabella sighed as if she'd seen it all a million times before. "Where did it come from?" she asked.

"I bought it for Labia," Hatcher told his mother, "but she doesn't want it."

"Give it to me," said the Countess, lifting the creature out of Celestia May's arms and stroking the back of its neck. "I'll look after it."

"But Father hates dogs," Hatcher pointed out.

"I know," smiled Isabella, and she took the dog downstairs to gleefully show it to her husband.

*

Making the most of his first day of industrial action, O'Donnell was lying on his bed listening to Muddleton FM, which was at that moment playing 'Annie I'm Not Your Daddy' by Kid Creole. He was suddenly disturbed by a terrible commotion coming from the beehive under his bed.

Anthogrid had finally returned from his near-fatal experience with the crab spider, and he wasn't looking forward to sharing news of the deaths of Arvid and Egil. But as he entered the hive, he soon realised that something far more important was going on. The queen was dead.

When a bee colony loses its queen, everyone knows right away, because hundreds of reporter bees start to gather outside the monarch's chamber and the queen no longer produces her unique and pungent aroma.

"I never liked that smell, anyway," said Anthogrid when he was told the sad news by one of the house bees. "What did she die of?" he asked.

"It was suicide," replied a house bee called Kjetil. "She was so bored, she stung herself in the face."

"I did not know that was a thing," replied Anthogrid. "So, what happens now, an election?"

The house bee laughed. "The queen has already given birth to her successors," he said. "The workers will put all her eggs in giant wax rearing cells and feed them with special food called royal jelly so they grow huge and fat."

"But how will we choose which one of them will be the next queen?" asked Anthogrid.

"We don't choose," explained Kjetil, "the first queen to emerge from her cell will kill all the other bees before they hatch."

Anthogrid could not help thinking that this was a little harsh. "What if two queens come out at the same time?" he asked.

Kjetil replied with relish. "Then the two rival queens battle it out to the death," he said. "If that happens, you really don't want to miss it. Book a front-row seat."

"I don't think I like being a bee," said Anthogrid.

*

Celestia May had been quite excited at the prospect of drowning a puppy. She hadn't performed any kind of sacrifice for several weeks, and she missed the feeling of well-being and fulfilment it gave her. Muddleton's witches' coven often made live sacrifices. They met once a week, on a Thursday, in a derelict canal barge which was moored in a dark and lonely spot on the River Turd. The Barge Coven had thirteen members and followed a strict code called the *Book of Shadows*. This contained religious texts, instructions for magical rituals and some very good recipes for fish.

The high priestess of the coven was a thin and unlovely woman called Dorothy Deadgoat, who believed herself to be a goddess and worked in a Little Chef on the A456 just outside Muddleton. The high priestess possessed strong psychic powers and heightened intuition and, as a result, had won the Health Lottery on three separate occasions. The priestess cast and purified the circle and invoked the spirits. She directed rituals, wrote chants and, most importantly, she brought along the sausage rolls.

Celestia May had been a member of the Barge Coven since she was fourteen years old. There was a three-degree system of advancement, each degree requiring a year and a day of study. Most of the witches didn't try very hard during the year and crammed all of their study into the day.

Huge, bubbling cauldrons were no longer used in the coven, and for convenience, spells were now usually cast using a small camping stove or a microwave oven. The live sacrifice that week was to be a young calf, which would be ritually trussed, throttled, stabbed and boiled. It was then cut up into veal chops and served with rosemary and black pepper. There was, however, a rumour going around the local Wicca community that a human baby might soon become available for sacrifice.

Down through the centuries, there had been many witches' covens in Muddleton. The most notorious was the Mulberry Witches, who operated during the time of Second Earl Jellico Rivers. They were a black-hearted congregation and would often steal infants from the village and sacrifice them in the woods. During their reign of terror, the population of Muddleton dropped by thirty-five per cent, and when they were finally arrested and tried in 1871, the community breathed a huge sigh of relief.

*

Melton Thornaby banged on the door of O'Donnell's room. "Give me the key to the wine cellar!" he bawled.

O'Donnell opened the door. "Can I help you, sir?" he said calmly.

"You cannot go on strike!" screamed Melton. "It's undemocratic."

"I am merely supporting my fellow staff," O'Donnell explained.

"Well, can't you support them after lunch?" ranted Thornaby.

"I'm afraid not," said O'Donnell, and he offered Melton a Polo mint. "Something to tide you over, sir," he said kindly.

"Right," said Melton, "I am taking matters into my own hands," and he clambered down the Great Staircase and made his way towards the Great Kitchen in the basement.

*

"But I hate dogs," cried Hardy, his piles getting ever more painful by the minute.

"I shall name him Sidney," announced Isabella, "after your father. Oh, look at his little face – he loves you."

"Get that bastard away from me," growled the Sixth Earl, "and go and find me some lunch!"

"I can't," explained Isabella, cuddling the puppy and kissing it on the nose, "Mrs. Frapp is attacking anyone who goes near the kitchen. She threw a wok at the African Queen."

"I wish you'd all stop calling him that," said Hardy. "He is genuine royalty. His father was a prince!"

"Then it is time he learnt some manners," said Isabella.

*

Nelly Frapp was sitting at the huge, rustic kitchen table, chopping carrots.

Melton burst in unannounced. "Aha! What are you doing?" he asked.

"I'm preparing lunch," replied the old lady.

"Excellent!" said Melton.

"It's not for you – it's for the staff," she snapped. "Now go upstairs and tell the Countess we're staying on strike 'til she gives the nanny her job back."

Melton tried to grab a carrot, but Mrs. Frapp stabbed at his hand with a carving knife. Its point dug deep into the tabletop, narrowly missing Thornaby's pinkie.

"I demand to be fed!" screamed Melton.

"Sod off!" said Mrs. Frapp.

Thornaby flicked his eyes around the Great Kitchen. There was half a loaf of granary bread on the marble top of the pinewood dresser. He lurched towards it, clutched it under his arm like a rugby ball and made a dash for the door.

"Stop right there," came a voice from behind him. Melton turned around. His eyesight wasn't very good, and he was wearing the wrong glasses, but he could just make out that the ninety-year-old cook was pointing a crossbow at him. He gently put the loaf onto the kitchen table, and saying nothing at all, he backed away slowly towards the door.

Nelly Frapp had an impressive collection of antique crossbows, and in case of emergency, she always kept one in the kitchen. The weapon she presently held in her hand was a medieval German crossbow, with an engraved stock and a lever trigger. It was after tripping over this particular crossbow, that Mrs. Frapp had accidentally fallen on her sword.

*

Dr. Rufus Dreyfuss responded to Hogg-Marchmont's phone call within an hour. He felt he owed the Sixth Earl an apology, but he had no idea why he was being summoned to Hogg Hall.

"You mustn't blame yourself," Hardy reassured him, "I told everyone to come to my funeral dressed as a chicken. It was just my little joke."

"Yes, but I was the only one stupid enough to do it," said Dreyfuss, "and I can only apologise for disrespecting your friends and your family name."

"I wholeheartedly accept your apology," smiled Hogg-Marchmont. "Now, will you please take a look at my anus?"

Dr. Dreyfuss was taken aback. "Your anus?" he replied.

"My anus," said the Sixth Earl.

"But I'm your dentist," said Dreyfuss, "why would I want to take a look at your anus?"

"Because I am no longer on friendly terms with my doctor," explained Hardy, "and I am in urgent need of the assistance of a medically trained professional."

Hogg-Marchmont had fallen out with his family GP some months before. He'd been playing golf with Dr. Theatre on the links near Muddleton Point and had been about to sink a short putt when the doctor's phone rang.

"Leave it!" snapped Hardy, but the doctor answered the phone and became embroiled in a forty-minute conversation about the intestinal tract of a Mrs. Snelling. By the time the game commenced, the light had faded, and Hardy had completely lost his concentration. He subsequently missed the crucial putt.

In the argument that followed, Hogg-Marchmont put up a strong case for golf being more important than the health of a patient, but Dr. Theatre was unable to agree with him and the pair had not spoken since.

Hogg-Marchmont dropped his trousers, and Dr. Dreyfuss peered hesitantly at his arse.

The dentist gagged. "It's haemorrhoids," he said.

"I know it's fucking haemorrhoids," blustered Hardy, "I just want you to put some cream on it."

"Can't your wife do that?" said the dentist weakly.

"No!" screamed the Sixth Earl.

Following an unsavoury incident with his university tutor, Dr. Dreyfuss had a deep-rooted loathing of the unclad human body. This was the principal reason he'd gone into dentistry, rather than general medical practice.

Hardy stood astride in the centre of the Great Sitting Room and bountifully spread the cheeks of his anus. At that precise moment, Nanny Alice came into the room. She feared to look, and yet she could not turn away.

"The Countess has agreed to give me my job back," she announced, her eyes glued to Hogg-Marchmont's hefty, pendulous testicles.

"Oh, for fuck's sake," sighed the Sixth Earl, "haven't you ever heard of knocking?"

The dentist bent over and, biting hard on his fist to stop his stomach from emptying, he prepared to apply ointment to Hardy's fully mature arse grapes.

"I'll do it," said Nanny Alice. "It's the least I can do."

For Hardy, to describe the events of the next few seconds would be an impossibility, were it not for the fact that he had a photographic memory. As Nanny Alice's cream-covered index finger moved towards his rump, the entire south wall of the Great Sitting Room suddenly crumbled to the ground, bringing a sizable section of the ceiling down with it. The aftershock sent Hardy, Dr. Dreyfuss and Nanny Alice toppling to the floor, and they crawled towards the door amid flying glass, falling timber and plaster. When the dust cleared away, Hardy could see the Hogg-Marchmont coat of arms laying shattered and splintered on the carpet.

By this time, the house was in pandemonium, people dashing back and forth in different directions. As O'Donnell waded through plaster to enter the room, there was another thunderous crash and a tremor like an earthquake gripped the whole house. A crack appeared and swiftly ran down the centre of the Great Sitting Room. Within seconds, it had widened to six feet. The Norwegian pine table toppled into it first, followed by the leather Chesterfield and the chaise longue. O'Donnell jumped clear just as the entire floor collapsed, and he helped Nanny Alice and Dr. Dreyfuss out into the hallway, where the three of them stood coughing and choking in the dust. Hardy still had his trousers around his ankles, but he somehow managed to shuffle out of harm's way and threw himself onto the carpet in the hallway. There was a thin trickle of blood coming from the hairline above his forehead.

The crash was heard as far away as the beer garden at the Pig & Pencil Case, where Muddleton Wine Society were having their weekly tasting. Melton Thornaby could tell right away that the sound had come from Hogg Hall. The resulting earth tremor had also dislodged the precariously balanced rock at Muddleton Point, and Ned the mallard had had a heart attack and slumped into the Great Fountain with a splosh.

*

That evening, his head bandaged, Hardy stood by the mantelpiece in the library. The Second Earl's Great Bohemian Chandelier had become dislocated by the seismic activity, and it now lay in ten thousand pieces in the centre of the floor, little shards of crystal glass everywhere.

"I've got the surveyor's report," Hardy told the family, "and it's not good. The council have booked the bulldozer for next Friday. We have just over a week to save Hogg Hall."

It wasn't raining in Muddleton, but it was raining as usual in the grounds of Hogg Hall. There was a steady *drip, drip, drip* into the plastic bucket in the centre of the Persian rug.

O'Donnell appeared at the door. "Mr. Dunn is here," he said.

"Dunn?" asked Hardy. "Who's Dunn?"

"Mr. Dunn from the Muddleton Morris Men," explained O'Donnell. "They've been searching for Master Keith in the north woods."

"Show him in," said Hogg-Marchmont grimly.

Dunn walked into the library and stood in front of the Great Mirror. "We've found something," he said.

Chapter Ten

The Muddleton Morris Men had found a body in the woods, but thankfully it was not the body of Master Keith. Forensic examination quickly revealed that the remains had been there since the late nineteenth century and were well preserved because of the high levels of peat in the forest soil. As soon as she heard of the discovery, Celestia May immediately knew how the child had ended up in its depthless grave. It had been a sacrifice of the Mulberry Witches, a coven of whom Celestia May's own high priestess Dorothy was an immense admirer.

*

Lord and Lady Ingleby-Barwick sat playing cards with Hogg-Marchmont in the Great Lounge, one of the few rooms in the house that had not suffered damage in the calamitous collapse of the previous day. Celestia May's houseplants loomed above the card table, and Hardy swore that he could see the giant trailing philodendron slowly edging its way along the mantelpiece. These robust plants were probably the only thing that was stopping the Great Lounge from collapsing too.

"How are your arse grapes?" enquired Ingleby-Barwick, ever concerned about the health of his friend.

"Painful," replied the Sixth Earl, "but that's the least of my problems, Angus. Thornaby's celebrity wine tasting is tomorrow, and it's going to be a fucking disaster. I wish I'd never agreed to it."

Ingleby-Barwick put down four aces and the king of hearts, and he dragged a pile of crumpled fivers towards himself. The pot had been running at a little over £200.

"Want to try and win it back?" he asked Hardy, but the Sixth Earl drained his brandy glass and slumped back into his armchair. He seemed deeply distracted.

"Maybe another day," he said. It wasn't like Hardy to not try and win back his losses.

"I called Celestia May's godfather Alessandro Alessandro this morning," said Hardy suddenly. "I've asked him to get rid of Prodding."

"Isn't that a bit rash?" replied Ingleby-Barwick, who did not approve of Hardy's Mafia connections.

"Do you have a better idea?" asked Hardy.

"As a matter of fact, I do," said Angus.

"I'm listening," said Hardy.

"Well, you know how much we all enjoy digging," he said.

"What of it?" asked Hardy.

"Well," suggested Ingleby-Barwick, "how about digging a moat?"

Quite apart from the recent shameful quarrying

episode at the beach, Angus had always been a big fan of digging holes, and it was not the first time he'd seen excavation as a solution to a problem. He lived in a spacious house that backed onto the north woods, and for many years, he'd been plagued by courting couples who would back their cars up to his rear fence and copulate noisily throughout the night. His solution was to hire a mechanical digger and sink a six-foot-deep trench, for a distance of about thirty yards, along the back of his property. He then covered the trench with netting, twigs and leaves. The following night, he managed to trap a VW Golf, a Honda Civic and two Ford Transit vans.

After incurring substantial bills for having their vehicles towed out of Angus's ditch, none of those vehicles ever returned, and news spread like wildfire that Ingleby-Barwick's rear passage was no longer a convenient location for a quick, backseat shag.

*

As was touched upon earlier in these chronicles, Angus had been quite a famous inventor in his day, and he was renowned for far more than just his Self-Ventilating Top Hat® and his Expandable Rotating Corset®. In the sixties, when smoky basement jazz clubs were at their most popular, many customers would often complain that there wasn't enough smoke in the club. Ingleby-Barwick therefore invented an Automatic Smoking Machine®, which was used to pump copious amounts of cigarette smoke or cigar smoke into music venues. The device also became popular during the early days of the alternative comedy circuit. Around the same time, Angus invented a Multipurpose Walking Stick®, which could instantly transform into an umbrella, a flute, a hockey stick, a horse measuring device or a net for capturing butterflies. There was also a vibrating version with three speed settings. Angus's Mechanical Feline Brush® won many awards – the device's various arms, hooks, gears and rotating surfaces allowing one to brush a cat without being in the same room with the creature. It was extremely popular among people with cat allergies. The downside was that around thirty per cent of the cats were decapitated during the grooming process, and the contraption was finally taken out of the shops in the late seventies.

Ingleby-Barwick's finest hour was probably his invention of solar-powered jewellery. Low-voltage lighting was placed within necklaces, bracelets and earrings, and a gigantic, flat solar panel was worn on the back. The panel rotated so that it always pointed at the sun, and the jewellery sparkled and shimmered like the constellations. Sadly, the invention received a lot of negative publicity, following a fashion event in Milan. Naomi Campbell was modelling one of Angus's low-voltage belly chains when the weight of the solar panel on her back sent her toppling off her ten-inch heels, and she landed in the lap of Karl Lagerfeld.

*

Hogg-Marchmont and Ingleby-Barwick, dressed as Marie Antoinette, burst into the saloon bar of the Pig & Pencil Case, which was playing Muddleton FM at full blast. Hardy raised his voice above the dulcet tones of Kid Creole singing the 1980's pop classic 'Stool Pigeon'.

"Drinks for everyone!" announced the late Sixth Earl, and there was a hearty cheer. Hogg-Marchmont had been a lot more generous since his death, and soon everyone was ordering at the bar.

"I'm looking for volunteers!" he announced, and the mood suddenly became more subdued. Many of the villagers had spent the last forty-eight hours combing the woods for Hardy's grandson, and there were only so many favours that Hardy could call in.

"We're going to build a moat!" exclaimed Hogg-Marchmont. "To stop those buggers from the council bulldozing Hogg Hall."

Old Mrs. Snelling, whose intestinal tract was now healing nicely, put up her hand. "I used to drive a V bucket digger," she said. "You can count me in."

Mrs. Snelling's bridge partner Mrs. Tibbins also put up her hand. She liked the Sixth Earl, even though his impromptu firework display had recently blown her hat off in the vegetable tent at the agricultural show.

"I'll help," said Mrs. Tibbins.

"Can you drive a digger?" asked Ingleby-Barwick.

"No," she replied, "but give me a shovel and a bucket, and I'll dig for England!"

"That's the spirit!" cheered Hogg-Marchmont, and before he knew it, he had a list of ten names.

*

Hardy and Ingleby-Barwick got quite drunk that evening, and as the clock in the parish church struck one, the pair found themselves crouched next to a wire fence in the centre of the village. Angus flashed his torch directly into his companion's eyes. Hardy had smeared dirt onto his face and looked like a British airman trying to escape from Stalag Luft III. On the other side of the fence, illuminated majestically by tungsten security lighting, was a bright yellow JCB 140 excavator, with caterpillar tracks. The African licked his lips. This monster could move a mountain of earth in no time at all. But it wasn't just about brute force; it was about precision, stability and torque.

"What's torque?" asked Hogg-Marchmont, but Angus didn't have time for a physics lesson. He was too busy slicing his way through the fence with a huge pair of wire cutters. The pair had considered hiring a digger but decided that the money was far better spent that evening in the pub. Instead, they would sneak into the building site over the road and steal the bugger. Mrs. Snelling, too, was hammered out of her skull.

"Are you sure you can drive this thing?" Hardy asked her.

"Piece of piss," said the old lady, emerging ghost-like from the shadows. She and the others stumbled through the hole in the fence. The JCB 140 had an anti-tamper device, an alarm and an advanced security management system, so it would be very hard to steal. But fortunately, the driver had left the door open and the keys in the ignition.

Mrs. Snelling was a koi carp fanatic and had designed and built many ponds in her time. In her younger days, she'd dug them by hand, but as she approached her seventy-fifth year, she'd become quite an expert at driving excavators. Her last pond had been almost twenty metres in diameter, so this JCB was a Dinky toy compared with some of the kit she'd hired.

Hogg-Marchmont had taken the precaution of snatching a bottle of single malt from behind the bar at the Pig & Pencil Case, and he and his two co-conspirators took it in turns to swig from it as Mrs. Snelling drove the JCB back towards Hogg Hall. There were only two near misses on the route home: one with an Audi, and one with a particularly thick-set badger, who appeared to do more damage to the JCB than the JCB did to it. The four-cylinder engine was pokier than you'd imagine, and as the JCB swerved onto the gravel drive of Hogg Hall, the speedometer was showing an impressive 63mph. The digger skidded to a halt with a handbrake turn, about three inches from the front door, and Mrs. Snelling immediately fell asleep at the wheel, switching on the headlights as she did so. Ingleby-Barwick climbed down from the cab and fell flat on his face.

Hardy weaved his way down to the observatory. He was much too excited to sleep. Instead, he sat and slowly sobered up, spending the early hours of the morning working out precisely where the Great Moat of Hogg Hall should be built. As the Sixth Earl walked back across the courtyard at 7am, five glowing lights, in delta formation, passed high over the house and disappeared into the eastern sky.

*

Hogg-Marchmont was awakened at 11am by his wife. "There appears to be a mechanical digger in the driveway," she said. "I don't suppose it's got anything to do with you."

Hardy was momentarily confused by this awakening, but then he remembered the plan. "We're going to dig a moat," he said.

The Countess tried to stay calm. "There is an elderly woman asleep inside the cab," she said.

"Don't worry," reassured the Sixth Earl, "that's Mrs. Snelling."

O'Donnell served brunch in the dining room, and Mrs. Snelling tucked in hungrily. She'd never been inside Hogg Hall before, and this was proving to be quite an adventure.

"We'll start digging right away," said Ingleby-Barwick. "How long have we got?"

"There's just over a week to go," replied Hardy. "It's going to be tight, but if all the volunteers show up, I think we can do it."

"It's diverting the water from the river that's going to be the tricky part," said Angus, "but I think I've worked out a way."

"You're a genius," said Hardy, and he slammed his hand hard onto his friend's back, knocking his spectacles flying in the process.

*

It was the day of Melton Thornaby's fundraising event, and he was down by the lake supervising the erection of an enormous marquee. It was raining as usual, and parts of the lawn were already turning into a quagmire. Event planning is a complex and challenging business. You need to prepare a budget and monitor your spending carefully. You need to arrange parking and easy access for your venue. There are sponsorship proposals to create, and flyers and posters need to be printed and distributed. Press releases are important, as are invitations, registration forms, food permits, promotional signage, lighting, PA systems, portable toilets, generators, public liability insurance and security. Thornaby had done none of these things. But he had told a few of his mates and put up a marquee.

"How's it going?" asked Hardy.

"We've had a few cancellations," replied Thornaby. "Nigella Lawson and Matt Baker have pulled out, but Biggins is still in."

"Oh good," said the Sixth Earl, "as long as we still have Biggins."

"What's the mechanical digger for?" asked Melton.

"Moat," explained Hogg-Marchmont.

"Splendid!" said Melton, and he took a sip from his hip flask.

Three hours later, the marquee was crammed with about three hundred guests. Word of mouth was a very powerful tool in Muddleton. Countess Isabella threw on a little black dress that turned out to be a lot tighter than the last time she'd worn it, and Lady Box-Girder wore a hat that appeared to have a magpie living in it.

"How kind of you to come," Isabella said to a journalist from the *Muddleton Gazette*.

"Oh, we always like to support events organised by the late Earl," he replied, and he drank a glass of Chablis so quickly that it was like watching a magician perform sleight of hand. Muddleton FM blared out one of Kid

Creole's lesser-known tracks, a rare platter called 'Dear Addy' which struggled to break into the top forty.

One end of the tent was stacked high with boxes of booze, supplied free of charge by Lidl, and the locals were doing their best to consume it in the shortest time possible. No one quite seemed to know if they were supposed to pay for their drinks, and now and again, Thornaby would wander around half-heartedly rattling a bucket and encouraging people to chuck loose change into it. Wearing wellington boots, the Morris Men were performing something quite sinister in the shallows of the lake, and Celestia May and her friends were sitting in a circle and cutting themselves with razor blades, while chanting something in a forgotten pagan language. There were no celebrities to be seen, B-list or otherwise.

Brother Tartaric from Ghastbury Abbey was giving an impromptu exhibition of grape treading, and Councillor Prodding was dutifully adding cress to Mrs. Frapp's egg sandwiches, all the while staring at the crumbling house with evil malice. Most inebriated seemed to be Mr. Crow, Registrar of Births, Deaths and Marriages, who was arm-wrestling with Mr. Mosely the undertaker. Dr. Dreyfuss was dressed as a grape. No one had asked him to do it, he just thought it would be appropriate for the occasion and would help to overwrite his chicken costume in the memories of Hardy's friends.

Viscount Hatcher picked up a hot rum punch from Mrs. Comerford and pushed his way past a newsreader from Muddleton FM.

"You've got a nerve," she snapped, "standing there drinking while your son is missing!"

Hatcher looked at the girl as if she was something stuck to the bottom of his shoe. Like all nobility, he had no real interest in the opinions of the great unwashed, particularly if they were journalists.

Thornaby, meanwhile, was doing his party trick. He lined up six bottles of wine on a trellis table, and each one had its label covered by a sock. Melton put on a blindfold and invited visitors to offer him sips of the wine, while he tried to guess the grape, the vintage and the vineyard.

"This is a Rioja," he said after sniffing and tasting the first one. "Alavesa vineyard. Firm, dark fruit flavours and notes of spice and dark chocolate."

"What year?" asked the visitor.

"2008," replied Melton. The sock was removed, and he was one hundred per cent incorrect. It was a French Merlot. He received a warm round of applause from the crowd. A second glass was poured. Melton took a long sip and sloshed it around his mouth. "This is a Rioja," he said. "2008. Firm black fruit flavours and notes of spice and dark chocolate." The sock was removed, and Melton was wrong again. It was a bottle of New Zealand Shiraz. More polite applause. Melton adjusted his blindfold, and someone passed him a glass from the third bottle. He took his time over this one, inhaling the bouquet attentively and taking a generous mouthful. There was a long pause.

"This is a Rioja," he said. "2008. Firm black fruit flavours and notes of spice and dark chocolate." The sock was removed, and it was a bottle of Tizer. Thornaby had been doing this routine for thirty years and was convinced that if he stuck with his strategy for long enough, he would one day come up with the correct answer.

As always, Mrs. Comerford seemed impressed by Melton's minor celebrity, and she winked at him flirtily and adjusted her surgical stockings when she knew he might be looking. On special occasions like this, Melton could generally rely upon Mrs. Comerford to round off his day.

By the time Christopher Biggins arrived, all the wine was drunk, as was Melton Thornaby. When Biggins complained, Thornaby took a swing at him and had to be restrained by Hardy and Ingleby-Barwick. While the pair were helping Melton to make a dignified exit, he lost his balance and fell heavily into the central tent pole, bringing the entire marquee crashing down around them.

Fighting broke out. Tiffany the midwife broke Councillor Bottomley's jaw, and James Cudd, the award-winning filmmaker, was thrown into the lake by two of the Muddleton Morris Men.

"Well, I think that went rather well," said Melton, and he headed for the Fingering Room in the Great Folly, where he had every intention of boffing Mrs. Comerford and then sleeping for at least twenty-four hours.

Meanwhile, fuelled by Melton's wine tasting, Mrs. Snelling had fired up the JCB and had already dug a trench about twenty yards long, ten feet wide and eight feet deep. Unfortunately, she'd dug it in the wrong place, and Hardy was now in the process of getting her to fill it in.

*

The next day, work began in earnest on building the moat. Ingleby-Barwick, wearing one of Maria's dresses from *West*

Side Story, helped Hogg-Marchmont stake out the path of the moat on the lawns surrounding the house. Meanwhile, Mrs. Snelling set to work with the JCB. Volunteers from the Pig & Pencil Case, now swollen to twenty-five, were issued with spades and buckets, and they started to dig like their lives depended on it. They and their ancestors had grown up with Hogg Hall. Many of their relatives had worked there, and they had no intention of watching it being knocked down. Nelly Frapp rustled up snacks, and O'Donnell grew steadily exhausted as he ferried wine back and forth from the cellar to help keep the workers well oiled and motivated. He'd had a restless and unsettling night. For the first time in months, there was no soothing buzzing noise coming from the beehive under his bed, and he'd become increasingly dependent on this sound to get to sleep.

*

Deep in the hive, Anthogrid awoke with a start, and he too was disturbed by the silence. He poked his head out of his hexagonal cell and looked around. The hive was deserted. There had been a meeting of the council the previous afternoon. Bees are very sensitive to vibration and geological movement, and it was becoming increasingly clear that Hogg Hall was no longer a safe place to live. With a new queen about to be crowned, and a higher birth rate than ever before, it was decided that the colony should move from the beehive under O'Donnell's bed and relocate to alternative accommodation. What with the frantic search for Master Keith, and preparations for the wine tasting, no one at Hogg Hall had noticed when, under the cover of evening twilight, the bees had made their move. They swiftly and efficiently vacated the hive, and after swirling around O'Donnell's bedroom to get their bearings, all forty thousound of them flew out through the open window and swarmed across the lake and into the woods.

Like most teenagers, Anthogrid lived in a world of his own, and news of the evacuation of the hive had failed to penetrate his bubble. He was also a very heavy sleeper, and by the time he woke up that morning, everyone had gone. The young bee sensed that the colony would head for the forest, so he wasted no time in darting out of the window and heading northwards. As he flew low over the dome of the observatory, he was suddenly filled with a rush of excitement. This was the first time he'd ever been on his own, and he found it exhilarating.

After zigzagging his way through the trees for a couple of hours, Anthogrid's nostrils were suddenly filled with a familiar and pungent aroma. It was the sweet perfume of a queen bee. He banked eastwards and flew towards the source of the smell. He soon realised that it was coming from within the hollow trunk of a vast tree.

Anthogrid's knowledge of thirteenth-century English history was sparse to say the least, and he had no way of knowing that this sprawling giant was the Great Henry Oak. As he flew towards it, he could hear a thousand drones humming 'Got To Get You Into My Life' by Earth Wind & Fire, and he knew that he had arrived at his new home.

Melton arose from the folly around midday, and he supervised as what was left of the marquee was dismantled, and the wreckage from the wine tasting was cleared away. The lawn by the lake looked like the aftermath of Glastonbury: bottles, glasses and litter strewn across the mud, and items of footwear and underwear all over the place.

"Did we raise any money?" Hardy asked Melton Thornaby.

Melton opened his wallet and took out a handful of crumpled notes. "It's all there," he said. "I think it's about forty quid."

"Thanks," said Hogg-Marchmont, and he stuffed it into the top pocket of his jacket.

*

There was a frenzy of excitement at the Barge Coven. Discovery of a human sacrifice from the days of the Mulberry Witches was cause for celebration, and the coven celebrated it like they celebrated everything else: by taking off their clothes and running around in circles screaming.

When everyone had calmed down a little, Celestia May approached Mrs. Deadgoat. Apart from a pair of Dr. Scholl's Wiley Wedge sandals, the high priestess was still naked. She was sweating profusely, and her pubic hair both resembled and moved like a large ball of tumbleweed.

"My brother's baby is still missing in the woods," said Celestia May. "I want to cast a spell to protect him."

"The child is ours," hissed the high priestess. "The Beast of the Woods has gathered it for us."

"No!" said Celestia May calmly. "There will be no sacrifice."

Mrs. Deadgoat knew she was in the presence of a more powerful witch. Although she was only seventeen, Celestia May was a potent force in the coven, and she was used to getting her own way.

"Very well," said the priestess. "We'll sacrifice a tortoise instead."

Mrs. Deadgoat opened the *Book of Shadows* and ran her finger down the index. "I shall cast a protection spell for the child," she said.

The high priestess knelt before the alter at the stern of the barge, and she placed an amethyst stone on it. She used a wooden twig to circle the stone in a clockwise direction, and she chanted in a voice not dissimilar to Kate Bush.

"To this charm I lend my part, to keep the child safe from harm,

"Lend the power from this stone to make him feel protection prone."

It was a bloody awful verse, but the sentiment was exactly what Celestia May was looking for.

"Thank you," she said.

"So mote it be," said the high priestess. "Anything else I can do for you?"

"Well, since you mention it," said Celestia May, "I don't suppose you know any curses for stopping a council bulldozer?"

Mrs. Deadgoat flicked through the index again.

"There's nothing under bulldozer," she said, "but I could do you a 'bring total chaos to your enemies,'" she said.

"That's close enough," said Celestia May. "Show me how to fight them. Show me how to defeat them."

The priestess tied three knots in a piece of string and recited another spell which we are not able to quote here in full, as it is far too dangerous, and there are probably copyright issues.

"So mote it be," said the high priestess when she'd finished reading it out.

"Transformation is coming!" chanted all thirteen members of the coven. "Regeneration for the ones who fly!"

At the end of the first day's digging at Hogg Hall, there was a deep, ten-foot-wide trench running the entire length of the south aspect. On the second day, two more mechanical diggers appeared mysteriously, and Mrs. Snelling quickly trained Hardy and O'Donnell to operate them. After three days and three nights, the team of volunteers had swollen to fifty-two, and a formidable trench, thirty feet wide, encircled the entire house. Ingleby-Barwick went into the library and began drawing up plans to divert water from the lake and flood the trench. There were now just four days until the council bulldozer arrived.

Chapter Eleven

Countess Isabella was awakened by something sitting on her face, and she was relieved to discover that it wasn't her husband. She lifted Sidney the puppy off the bed and watched as he gleefully pissed over her slippers. Before the creature had a chance to deposit solids in the rest of her footwear, she threw on a coat, picked him up and headed for the lawn.

As soon as Isabella put the dog down, he took off across the grass and was soon snuffling around in the weeds and bulrushes that surrounded the lake. He'd obviously got scent of something, and it was something with a very strong smell indeed.

*

Now dressed in an admiral's dress uniform, complete with bi-corner hat, Lord and Lady Ingleby-Barwick had now calculated that in order to complete the defensive moat around Hogg Hall, the mechanical diggers would have to excavate a long, narrow gully from the south shore of the lake to the circular trench that now surrounded the house, a distance of roughly one hundred yards.

"Do you think we can do it in four days?" asked the Sixth Earl.

"I think we can do it in three days," replied Angus.

Straight after breakfast, the JCBs fired up, and digging began. Hogg-Marchmont began to feel for the first time that there might actually be some hope of stopping the council bulldozer in its tracks and saving Hogg Hall from demolition.

*

The Countess hadn't taken a dog for a walk since she was a little girl, and she began to feel quite warm and fuzzy inside, a sensation that she rarely experienced living at Hogg Hall. She and Sidney walked past the observatory and along the east shore of the lake. When they reached the north side, the puppy bounded around behind the folly and disappeared into semi-darkness beyond the treeline.

"Sidney!" called out the Countess, but the animal had absolutely no idea what a Sidney was. Indeed, he didn't know what anything was, and he certainly had no intention of returning to his mistress in the near future. Isabella followed the puppy into the woods, and she soon wished that she'd put on a sturdier pair of shoes.

"Sidney!" she called out again, but the dog had disappeared from sight. Then something very unusual happened. The dawn chorus was in full swing, and blackbirds, chaffinches, blue tits and wood pigeons were loudly competing for airtime. But without warning, every single bird in the woodland stopped singing.

That's odd, thought the Countess. Then there was a low grunt, followed by a resonant snarl, followed by a thunderous, ear-splitting roar. Isabella heard a distant whimper from the puppy and then the sound of something massive stampeding through the undergrowth and into the distance.

The Countess's first instinct was to run away, but instead, she found herself pushing further and further into the woods. After a few more paces, she spotted Sidney. Surprisingly, he was unharmed, and the dog was sniffing at what looked like a nest on the forest floor. The Countess approached cautiously. The nest was elaborately woven of twigs and lined with moss, and in the centre of it was her grandson. Master Keith looked safe and well, and he was smiling peacefully in his sleep.

"Oh my god," whispered Isabella, and she picked him up gently. The baby seemed well fed, and he smelt clean and newly bathed. There was a little freshly dined breast milk around his lips.

Isabella dashed back towards the house, the puppy scampering along behind her. As she crossed the lawn, the sun came out for exactly four seconds, before shrinking back behind a dark, grey cloud.

News of the baby's safe return brought the whole family together in the Great Lounge, and even the giant houseplants seemed pleased that Master Keith was safe. Celestia May thought the Madagascar dragon tree looked particularly happy.

Lady Labia Antoinette held the infant tightly, and every time Nanny Alice tried to take her away, she hissed and said a curse word in French. Viscount Hatcher seemed less concerned about his son's health and more concerned about who or what had abducted him.

"What the Hell is in those woods?" he yelled. "I say we go down there and burn it out."

"Whatever it is, it brought the baby back safely," said Celestia May. "It's a noble beast and we should be protecting it, not hunting it."

"But why did it take the baby in the first place?" asked Melton.

"Perhaps it's lonely," said Ingleby-Barwick, and he glanced out of the window to see how the excavations were getting on. At that moment, the baby growled as loudly as a bear, taking everyone by surprise and prompting Thornaby to spit out a mouthful of Chilean Merlot. Hardy studied the infant, which now seemed to have rather more hair on its body than seemed apt.

"I remember when you were that size," he said to Hatcher in a guarded outburst of sentimentality. But he was lying. He didn't remember anything at all about Hatcher's childhood. When his son had taken his first steps, Hogg-Marchmont had been in Wormwood Scrubs. On Hatcher's first day at school, Hardy was having his stomach pumped in a rehab unit in Johannesburg, and when his son started at university, the Sixth Earl was on trial at the Old Bailey for allegedly plotting to kidnap Baroness Tanni Grey-Thompson.

The incident with the pillow in Hardy's bedroom was not the first time Hatcher had contemplated killing his father. Even in a house the size of Hogg Hall there is only enough room for one alpha male, and in some ways, it was a miracle that Hogg-Marchmont had survived into his late fifties. During their lifetimes, none of the five Earls had got on with their heirs, and it was only in death that they'd become united in a common cause.

The Third Earl, for example, was furious when he discovered that his son Kenneth was a homosexual, and he had once attempted to murder him in the library, first with a poker and then with a double-headed Norse battleaxe.

Lady Labia Antoinette pushed her way through the lounge's dense shrubbery and went and sat on an Edwardian drop-arm sofa. She took out her breast to feed Master Keith, and the baby clamped his mouth onto her nipple. After only a few gulps, he pulled his head away and made a sound that sounded distinctly like *Yuk!* Lady Labia tried to push his head back, but he screamed lustily and then puked over his mother. During his forest adventure, the infant had obviously become accustomed to a more palatable brand of mammal milk, unpolluted by gin, food additives and over-the-counter medication.

*

Hardy was increasingly fascinated by Nanny Alice, and the more she repelled his flirtations, the more determined he became to romance her. She had, after all, finally agreed to apply ointment to his haemorrhoids and greater love hath no woman than that.

"I know it wasn't your fault," he said to her quietly. "How were you to know what was going to happen?"

Alice narrowed her eyes. She was happy that the Sixth Earl laid no blame at her door, and yet at the same time, she was perfectly aware of his motives. She smiled at Hardy, and he smiled back. Many male aristocrats have an unhealthy attraction towards nursery nurses, and this is usually because their first sexual experience was with their own nanny. When he was just eleven years old, Hardy's nanny had shown him how to interfere with himself, and he therefore found the sight of a crisply pressed apron almost unbearably arousing. Nanny Alice, of course, knew of this well-trodden pattern of behaviour. She'd slept with almost all the fathers of her young charges, and with one or two of their mothers as well. She noticed Hardy looking at her again and adjusted her apron. The Sixth Earl blushed, and his tiny ears turned bright red.

*

At Muddleton constabulary, Sergeant Foot was in the briefing room with WPC Foreman-Grill and PC Hardmeat.

"That's three JCB excavators reported stolen in the past week," he said. "Now, what would a criminal do with three mechanical diggers?"

PC Hardmeat used all his powers of deduction. "Dig three holes?" he suggested.

"Good insight," said Foot. "Now, get in that patrol car, and drive around until you see three holes."

"What if we see two holes?" asked PC Hardmeat.

At Muddleton Council Chambers, the mayor was having a good day. He was about to flatten Hogg Hall to the ground, and life didn't get any better than that. Councillor Prodding was a cunt, but there was a fairly good reason for that observation. At school, he had been bullied because his long trousers were almost as short as everyone else's short trousers. He had also started to go bald at the age of eight and had sported a full beard since turning twelve. Prodding had worked at the town hall since leaving school at sixteen and quickly realised that the only way he was going to avoid being bullied was to work his way up to the top. Being unpopular is a huge disadvantage in most professions, but it's a positive advantage if you work in local politics.

The mayor stood in the car park admiring his favourite bulldozer. It was a Komkatzi D475 Bastard – a colossal eleven hundred-horsepower monster, capable of moving over 150 cubic yards of rubble with a single push of its huge ripper. It was the largest bulldozer in production, and thanks to Prodding, it had demolished Grade I-, Grade II- and Grade III-listed buildings all over Muddleton. It would make short work of Hogg Hall.

Councillor Prodding loved demolition. Earlier that year, he'd demolished a fourteenth-century abbey because it had insufficient baby-changing facilities, and there had also been widespread press coverage of his destruction of the much-loved Muddleton Point lighthouse, because Prodding said it was too tall and 'spoilt the sea view from the town hall'.

The mayor was excited to be personally riding the bulldozer to Hogg Hall that morning, and his hatred of Hardy Hogg-Marchmont went far beyond their short but well-documented argument concerning cress. Even though Hardy barely knew who Councillor Prodding was, in the mayor's mind, he had been at war with the Sixth Earl ever since Hogg Hall's owner had failed to get the necessary planning permission to build his observatory. Needless to say, the Hogg-Marchmonts had never sought permission to build anything, and they had no intention of starting now. The First Earl didn't ask anyone if he could divert the River Turd. He just bought twenty tons of dynamite and got on with it. The Second Earl built the Great Folly on a whim. He considered the whim to be his own private property, and he was certain that he could build on it any time he liked.

Councillor Prodding put his arm around his Head of Demolition, Todd Manshaft, and gave him an ebullient squeeze.

"Looking forward to it?" he asked.

"Stoked," replied Todd, through gritted teeth.

Manshaft didn't even like being hugged by his own mother and strongly believed there was no longer a place in the modern workplace for any kind of squeeze, ebullient or otherwise. Prodding, however, was very fond of the ebullient squeeze. He had once given one to Her Majesty the Queen and had been wrestled to the ground by four less-than-ebullient security men.

The bulldozer's driver, known simply as Pitbull, put the behemoth into gear, and it rumbled out of the car park of the town hall, removing the nearside bumpers of a number of vehicles as it did so. It was a short drive to Hogg Hall, and on the way there, the bulldozer accidentally took out a nineteenth-century drystone wall, two medieval cow sheds and a pre-Christian stone circle which had stood on the outskirts of Muddleton since 2000 BC.

It wasn't long before the vehicle turned off the main road, went through the pig-adorned main gates and began to thunder up the gravel drive of Hogg Hall. It narrowly missed the estate car of Lady Prunella Box-Girder, who was just parking up on the gravel drive, her car radio blaring out 'I'm a Wonderful Thing, Baby' by Kid Creole & the Coconuts. She loved the band's fusion of Latin and disco, and her stereo had been locked to Muddleton FM for many years.

Lady Prunella received fewer and fewer invitations to social events these days, and so the demolition of a prominent stately home was an occasion not to be missed. Prunella had bought a special hat for the day. It was an ebony, wide-brimmed, straw trilby, trimmed with black fishnet veiling and floating, multicoloured crystals. It perched on her head at a jaunty angle that said, "I know this is a sad occasion, but I'm here to support you, and I want everyone to look at me."

Teetering on a pair of ankle cuff sandals with seven-inch heels, Lady Prunella made her way towards the small crowd gathered outside Hogg Hall.

During the past few days, Hogg-Marchmont's mechanical diggers had made spectacular progress. The water from Ingleby-Barwick's clever new sluice gates at the lake now filled the newly excavated gully, but it could not complete its journey into the defensive moat because the diggers had hit an obstruction: a seam of solid granite.

"I'm sorry," Ingleby-Barwick told Hardy, "I should have surveyed the ground before we started digging, but there was no time."

"It's not your fault," said the Sixth Earl, "it's just bad luck."

*

Even as the bulldozer appeared at the gates, Mrs. Snelling's JCB was still trying to smash its way through the rock, and Hogg Hall's defences remained incomplete.

"How long to break through it?" asked Hogg-Marchmont.

Ingleby-Barwick thought hard. "Two weeks?" he said.

"We don't have two weeks," Hardy sighed.

The Sixth Earl needed time alone. He walked across to the Great Tithe Barn and sat on a hay bale. He was hoping that the white owl would be there for company, but it was nowhere to be seen. Hardy kicked off his shoes, put his feet up and closed his eyes. Had he done enough to delay the demolition of Hogg Hall, or was he just jerking off? He heard someone come into the barn, which was weird because almost no one ever went in there. He felt a pair of warm hands rest gently on his shoulders, and he opened his eyes. It was Nanny Alice.

Back at the house, Lady Prunella seemed disappointed that refreshments were not being served. She went and chatted to Ingleby-Barwick, who was the only brown man she had ever met.

"When does it start?" she said.

"When does what start?" asked Angus.

"The demolition," she said. "I thought it would be well under way by now. I have to be back in the village for a hair appointment at five."

*

On the other side of the north woods, at the Great Henry Oak, Anthogrid had now fully developed into an adult bee. He and his newest friend Osvald were on their way to Hogg Hall to forage for nectar in the wildflower beds that surrounded the West Wing. They hovered briefly over the turret of the folly, before whizzing across the lake and heading towards the house. His wings now fully developed, Anthogrid showed off his flying skills and swooped low over the courtyard. There had never been any kind of obstacle there before and, losing his concentration for an instant, he flew straight into the face of the mayor, who was posing for a selfie next to the bulldozer.

The head of the council swiped at Anthogrid angrily, and on the second swipe, he caught him with the back of his hand. The bee span out of control and landed with a plop on the gravel drive. He was stunned for a moment but quickly pulled himself together and was about to take to the air again.

"Look out!" screamed Osvald, but it was too late. Prodding's foot stamped down hard, and within a split second, Anthogrid was dead.

"You shouldn't have killed that bee," said Pitbull.

Osvald hovered around the mayor's head, staring in disbelief at the crushed remains of his foraging partner.

Surely there had been more to Anthogrid's destiny than this. His short life had seemingly been leading up to something meaningful, something far-reaching, something significant, but now he lay squashed like a grape on the gravel drive of Hogg Hall, and no one gave a shit. Osvald said goodbye to his friend, turned northwards and headed back towards the bees' nest at the Great Henry Oak.

*

Rearranging his trousers as he slipped out of the Great Tithe Barn, Hardy was delighted to see that the fifty or so volunteers from the village were now standing in a line on the south side of the trench, and some of them were angrily waving their picks and shovels at the council men. Pitbull replied by giving them the finger, and Todd just smiled a thin Clint Eastwood smile and lit a slim cigar. He was the demolition expert with no name, and his name was Todd Manshaft.

"Can you get across that trench?" Prodding asked Pitbull.

"No problem," said the driver, "the banks are not too steep." He put the bulldozer into gear.

Pitbull was right. Without being filled with water, the moat offered little or no defence at all to this caterpillar-tracked brute.

Hardy looked up at the sky, as if asking for divine guidance, and at that moment, five golden lights once again soared over the lake and circled above the house. To the deafening sound of huge flapping wings, the five Earls landed on the roof, and Marvel Comic-like, they arranged themselves into an offensive line along the escarpment overlooking the courtyard.

"Am I the only one who can see that?" Hardy murmured under his breath, and a voice from behind him said, "No."

It was Celestia May. "I can see them too," she said.

Hardy's dead father tapped his nose and waved to his granddaughter. The Fourth Earl looked down and saluted in true Luftwaffe style, and the Third Earl tipped his top hat in polite greeting. Earls one and two were both fighting drunk and more than ready for a punch-up.

The bulldozer moved closer to the edge of the trench, and Councillor Prodding produced a megaphone.

"Tell all these people to go home!" he demanded. "We don't want anyone to get hurt."

Prodding was in his element. "Doesn't this thing go any louder?" he asked Manshaft.

Todd turned the setting on the mouthpiece from 'Huge Dick' to 'Massive Arsehole', and the mayor's voice boomed out even more powerfully than before.

"You are hereby informed," announced Prodding, "that the aforementioned property 'Hogg Hall' has been deemed an unsafe structure according to article 27F of Muddleton Planning and Building regulations and has been scheduled for demolition with immediate effect."

There was a ripple of ironic applause from the assembled villagers, and a man from the darts team at the Pig & Pencil Case blew a raspberry.

"In the interest of public safety," Prodding continued, "we will ensure that all work is carried out safely. Residents of the said building must vacate the property and its surrounding area on presentation of this order."

At the end of this rousing little speech, Councillor Prodding had to genuinely restrain himself from shouting, "Unleash Hell!"

On the north side of the defences, the Muddleton Morris Men suddenly appeared from nowhere and assembled themselves in front of the bulldozer. Led by old Ben Dunn, they began to work their way through Lionel Bacon's *Handbook of Morris Dances*, starting with the Burton Stather Broom Dance.

Todd tapped his feet in time to the music, but Prodding shoved him, and he stopped. Pitbull put the bulldozer back into gear and edged it forward, but the Morris Men's defence stayed solid, and they simply changed formation and went into the Pilgrim's Charm Sword Dance.

Ignoring the presence of Prunella Box-Girder, Countess Isabella came and stood close to her husband and held his hand in a gesture of support and defiance.

"The nerve of the woman," she hissed under her breath, but at the same time she felt a trifle underdressed. Hardy smiled at his wife then glanced up at the five Earls perched on the balustrade, their wings silhouetted against a Titian sky. When Hardy next checked on the progress of the bulldozer, thirteen witches stood in a semi-circle on the south side of the trench. They stood close to the granite rock that was holding back the waters from the lake. Each one was holding a bouquet of heather and henbane.

Finally grasping that demolition of the house was imminent, Lady Labia Antoinette came running out of Hogg Hall with a few belongings thrown hastily into a suitcase. Then she turned and ran back into the house, realising that she'd forgotten the baby.

"Shall I run the morris dancers over?" asked Pitbull.

"You'd better not," replied the head of the council. "They're the lifeboat crew as well."

O'Donnell appeared on the house side of the trench holding two loaded duelling pistols, and next to him stood Mrs. Frapp, her crossbow trained on the forehead of Councillor Prodding.

Witches' brooms can be used to stir the winds in the sky, and they can also conjure rain or summon thunder. Although there are many plants that have 'water-bringing' properties, it's a mixture of moorland heather and the poisonous herb henbane that is most powerful. Allied with the realms of mist and rain, they are both excellent herbs to include in a water spell. Celestia May led the chant, as the high priestess Mrs. Deadgoat raised her hands to the heavens. A tiny storm cloud began to form directly overhead. As the witches repeated the water spell for the thirteenth time, a single fork of lightning crashed down from above, and the granite stone split in two, sending shards of rock flying everywhere.

The volunteers from the village waved their spades in the air and cheered as millions of gallons of water were suddenly unleashed, and a high-pressure deluge flowed forth into the moat. Churning and bubbling like rapids, the water quickly swirled around the entire circumference of the moat, and it was only a few seconds before the house was encircled in a formidable halo of deep water.

"Ladies and gentlemen," announced Hardy, "the Great Moat of Hogg Hall."

The Sixth Earl ran over to Ingleby-Barwick and threw his arms around him.

"Nicely done, sir!" he said in his ear.

"I think you had better thank your daughter," Angus replied, and he watched as the water in the moat glistened in the weak, mid-morning light.

"Just one thing," Hardy asked.

"What's that, old man?" said Angus.

"How do we get out of here?" enquired the Sixth Earl.

Angus looked at the access road on the other side of the moat and then behind him at the front door of Hogg Hall. "Zip wire?" he said.

That was good enough for Hogg-Marchmont, and he marvelled at his friend's seemingly never-ending optimism and inventiveness.

"I'd pay to see Mrs. Frapp on a zip wire," said Hardy.

Pitbull turned off the engine of the bulldozer. "What do we do now?" he asked.

"We will attack from the air," replied the mayor. "I know a man with an ex-RAF Lancaster bomber. We'll hire it and drop explosives on the house."

"I'm not sure that's legal during peacetime," Manshaft pointed out, and he began to wonder if Prodding was entirely sane. His boss had, after all, once dropped a thousand tons of cress onto the offices of *Farmer's Weekly*.

Forthwith, the mayor looked upwards, and the sky was at once filled with bees. Led by Osvald, the swarm whirled in a menacing spiral around the bulldozer, and by the time Prodding and Manshaft had wound up the windows, there were already thousands of angry bees inside the cab.

"I recognise those bees," said O'Donnell, and he noticed that the creatures were only attacking the men from the council and completely ignoring everyone else who was gathered outside Hogg Hall.

"How can you recognise a bee?" asked Hatcher.

"They used to live under my bed," said O'Donnell.

Ten minutes later, all but one of the bees had returned to the Great Henry Oak, the missing bee having been unwisely eaten by the Countess's puppy.

Pitbull and Manshaft staggered from the bulldozer, their bodies covered with excruciating stings. Councillor Prodding lay dead on the floor of the cab, his head like a giant swollen tomato, his heart stopped from severe anaphylactic shock.

Pitbull looked at his body. "I told you that you shouldn't have killed that bee," he said.

*

Osvald sensed that it would have been better if he'd died, and Anthogrid had led the attack on the bulldozer, but the universe is far too disorganised a place to be concerned about neat conclusions to the journeys of heroes.

A long, black limousine skidded to a halt on the gravel drive, and Alessandro Alessandro climbed out. He was unable to cross the moat, so he called Hardy on his mobile. "OK, which of these punks is Prodding?" he asked.

"The dead one," replied Hardy.

"He's already dead?" exclaimed Celestia May's godfather. "That is extremely disappointing."

"Sorry," said the Sixth Earl.

"You want I should kill someone else?" asked the gangster.

Hardy felt genuinely embarrassed that he had no one for the Mafia man to murder. He'd come a long way. He briefly considered putting out a contract on Laurence Llewelyn-Bowen but decided against it.

"Can I take a rain check?" asked Hardy.

"No problem," said Alessandro Alessandro, and he climbed back into his car and drove off. The Sixth Earl stood and stared at Hogg Hall. All at once, he understood that the more damaged, distressed and derelict the house became, the more beautiful it appeared to him. Even as he had this realisation, there was a loud crack, and another of the pig gargoyles detached itself from the north facade and crashed onto the gravel drive.

As if taking their cue from this event, amid the sound of mighty beating wings, the five Earls took to the air. They were satisfied with what they'd seen. Against all the odds, the Sixth Earl had proved himself worthy of the name Hogg-Marchmont. Hardy waved farewell to his father for the sixth time; the statue of Polyclitus gave him the skunk eye; and two hundred cats appeared out of nowhere and filed back into Hogg Hall. With the *nee-nah* of approaching police sirens echoing in their ears, everyone went into the house for a glass of wine.

Melton Thornaby, who'd been having forty winks in the Great Lounge, appeared in the entrance hall, stretching and yawning.

"Did I miss anything?" he asked.

Chapter Twelve

In the event of Councillor Prodding's grisly demise, the town council decided that destruction of Hogg Hall should be postponed, at least for the time being. Which was music to the ears of Hardy Hogg-Marchmont. Meanwhile, the Sixth Earl's file was no doubt passed once again to the Crown Prosecution Service.

The Great Moat having been so hastily excavated, it at first featured no bridge, or indeed any means of crossing it at all, and Ingleby-Barwick's inventive talents were quickly called upon to construct some means of traversing from the house to the access road and the front drive. His original idea of a zip wire proved too hazardous, but it took he and a few of the villagers only a few days to fashion a footbridge, using rubble from the recently collapsed East Wing.

It was now a fairly regular occurrence for Hogg-Marchmont and Nanny Alice to tiptoe across this little bridge after dark and make their way down to the Fingering Room in the Great Folly, where they would entertain one another in special ways.

It was almost 10am when Melton Thornaby finally appeared in the Great Dining Room. Dressed as Julius Caesar, Ingleby-Barwick sat next to the Sixth Earl. They were both already tucking into the most important meal of the day.

"Where have you been?" asked Hardy. "It's not like you to be late for breakfast."

Melton sat down at the dining table, tucked a napkin into the top of his shirt and popped a piece of black pudding into his mouth. "I thought I'd go for a walk to work up an appetite," he explained. "I've just had a very pleasant stroll around the stable block."

"Stable block?" replied Hardy. "We haven't got a stable block."

"Well, not since it burned down," added Ingleby-Barwick, striking a regal pose and showing off his enviable knowledge of the history of Hogg Hall.

Even though it was destroyed almost thirty years before he was born, Hardy was very familiar with the stable block, as there was a splendid painting of the building above the sideboard in the dining room. This impressive outbuilding was added to Hogg Hall by the First Earl in 1801. It was a two-storey building, in the Georgian style, constructed around a magnificent central courtyard. Above the elegant arched entrance was a clock tower with a bell inside it and a weather vein on the top of a stylish little domed turret. The wind sail was of glinting, polished brass and was forged into the shape of a rampant warthog.

The stable block was consumed by fire in 1928, when the young Kenneth Hogg-Marchmont, while taking his first flying lesson, accidentally flew a Curtiss P-1 Hawk into it. Due to quick thinking by staff, all the animals were rescued, but being unable to afford to rebuild it, the Fourth Earl levelled the stables to the ground.

Melton Thornaby laughed. "Well, if there's no stable block, what was that big building I just walked around?"

Hardy got up from the table and looked out of the west-facing window. He let out a scream.

"Good grief, Hardy, whatever is the matter?" asked Ingleby-Barwick.

Hardy said nothing. He just stood looking out of the window, his jaw hanging open.

Ingleby-Barwick dabbed his mouth with a napkin, got up and walked across to the window, where he, too, stood looking stunned. Too hungry to take any notice of what was going on, Melton filled his plate with sausages and tucked in.

The big wooden door creaked open, and Countess Isabella came into the Great Dining Room. She, too, had just looked out of a west-facing window on the first floor and appeared as shocked as if she had seen a ghost. She joined Hardy and the African at the window, and the three of them together stared in disbelief. The First Earl's stable block had returned. It seemed that Hogg Hall was beginning to restore itself.

*

"I suppose this has something to do with you," Countess Isabella said to her daughter as she and the entire family stood in the courtyard of the First Earl's miraculously rebuilt stable block.

"We did cast a restoration spell," replied Celestia May a little guiltily, "but I'm sure white magic is not powerful enough to do something like this."

"We can't afford a stables!" yelled the Countess. "Oh, God, I am so sick of this place!" She glared at Hardy. She could not yet think of a way of blaming him, but she would come up with something.

Viscount Hatcher was also finding it hard to get his head around this, but then again, he found it hard to get his head around anything.

"So, one minute there are no stables at Hogg Hall, and now there are stables," he pondered.

Meanwhile, completely unaware of the mystical events of that morning, Lady Labia Antoinette sniffed at the fresh aroma of horse manure on the breeze. "What is smelly?" she asked.

Melton Thornaby was the least surprised of anyone. He had quite simply never noticed that there wasn't a stable block at Hogg Hall. He looked up at the clock on top of the stables. "It's three minutes slow," he pointed out. This actually wasn't bad, since it hadn't been wound for almost ninety years.

"So, if it wasn't the witches' doing," reasoned Hardy, "then it would appear that Hogg Hall has decided to start rebuilding itself."

"But we don't need stables," cried Isabella. "If the house is bent on self-restoration, why doesn't it start by rebuilding the Sitting Room or the Orangery? Or, how about putting up a few new tiles in the kitchen?"

"The stables were the first part of the house to be destroyed," reasoned Celestia May. "So, Hogg Hall may be rebuilding itself in chronological order."

"But it's a house!" screamed Hatcher, his cheek hairs bristling. "How can a house repair itself?"

O'Donnell appeared, carrying a tray of Pimm's.

"This is no ordinary house," he said, "this is Hogg Hall."

*

Of course, in the late eighteenth century, the stables at Hogg Hall were not used for horses. In those days, it was the custom to tame and ride the giant sapphire stags who were then plentiful in the north woods, and on the heather moorlands that stretched westwards from Muddleton Point. It was a great skill to capture and break a stag and an even greater skill to persuade the beast to be saddled and ridden like a thoroughbred. Many trainers and riders died in the process, but the greatest trainer of them all was Lazarus Egg. A tanned and vigorous man who looked a lot younger than his fifty years, Egg worked for the First Earl, whose saddled stags were in great demand by noblemen all over the county.

*

It was a crisp, autumn day in 1791 and Lazarus Egg rode like the wind through the north woods, his thick, white hair swept back on the breeze, his strong hands grasping tight onto the reigns of his powerful mount. There is no more magnificent sight than a fully grown sapphire stag galloping through the trees, its mighty antlers thrust upwards, its rider clad in a red hunting jacket and white gloves.

Lazarus Egg was by far the most accomplished stag rider in the kingdom, but he did not see the tree branch coming until too late. The stag ducked just in time, but the overhanging branch struck Lazarus square on the forehead, sending him flying backwards out of the saddle. He landed with a thump in a pile of leaves. The stag reared up and flashed a bright eye over its shoulder, to see what had happened to its master.

Everything went black, and Lazarus Egg fell unconscious for what seemed an eternity. When he opened his eyes, the stag was gone. The disorientated rider stood up and looked around him, wondering how long he'd been out. He tentatively felt for the wound on his head but, to his surprise, it had already healed. As Lazarus Egg walked southwards through the woods, he saw many strange things. First, he noticed that all the trees had grown, not by just a few inches but some by more than twenty or thirty feet. Next, Lazarus encountered the Great Folly on the north side of the lake. Could this monstrosity really have been constructed while he was unconscious? But worse was to come. As he walked across the north lawn, he noticed that the entire East Wing of Hogg Hall was gone, and turning into the courtyard of the stables, he was horrified to see that all his beloved stags had disappeared.

Hatcher and Lady Labia Antoinette were sitting in the dining room eating lunch when Lazarus Egg walked in.

"Who the Hell are you?" snapped Hatcher. "How did you get in here?"

Lazarus said nothing. He just looked very puzzled, turned around and slowly shuffled back out into the hall.

"It must be another of your father's awful drinking companions," said Lady Labia, and she shovelled some yellow mush into the baby's mouth. It burped like a walrus and frowned at its mother with the eyes of a beast.

"Well, I haven't seen him around here before," said Hatcher, and he rang the bell for O'Donnell.

"Who was that man?" he enquired of the servant.

"I believe that was Mr. Lazarus Egg," replied O'Donnell, who was of course familiar with the portrait of Egg that hung in the Great Sitting Room.

"Egg?" blurted Hatcher. "What kind of name is that?"

"Forgive me, sir," said O'Donnell, "but I think you'll find it is a very famous name in these parts."

His whole life, Hatcher had not listened to anything he'd been taught at Hogg Hall, and that's why he was as stupid as a spoon.

Lazarus next encountered Celestia May who also immediately recognised him from his portrait.

"Welcome back," she said calmly. Celestia May wasn't sure if Lazarus Egg was a ghost or a time traveller, but she didn't really think it mattered very much as it amounted to the same thing. "Shall I tell the Sixth Earl you're here?" she asked, wondering if she was the only one who could see him.

"The Sixth Earl?" he asked. "What do you mean the Sixth Earl? Where is the First Earl?"

Next to the portrait of Egg was a huge painting of the First Earl and five companions, each in full hunting garb and mounted on massive sapphire stags. They were in pursuit of a tiny, terrified fox who had been sketched in, almost as an afterthought, in the corner of the composition. Having been painted before the invention of photography, the artist had of course represented the galloping of the stags completely incorrectly, their front and rear legs stretched out in almost straight lines.

Hardy, Angus and Thornaby stood staring at the painting.

"I'm sorry, old man," said Melton, "but I'm afraid you're going to have to run that past me again."

Hardy put his hand around Thornaby's shoulders and gave him a manly squeeze. "We are going to learn how to ride stags," he said.

"Why?" asked Ingleby-Barwick, fairly unfazed by this suggestion.

"Because," said Hardy, "Hogg Hall wants us to. Just like our ancestors."

"Looks fucking dangerous to me," observed Thornaby, closely inspecting the painting.

"It is dangerous," announced Hogg-Marchmont, "and that's exactly why we're going to do it."

"No Hogg-Marchmont has ridden a stag for over two hundred years," Ingleby-Barwick pointed out, once again showing off his encyclopaedic knowledge of the history of Hogg Hall.

"But now we have a teacher," explained Hardy, pointing at the adjacent portrait on the wall. "We will be taught to ride sapphire stags by Lazarus Egg."

Ingleby-Barwick studied the painting of Egg. "But he's dead," he said.

"Not anymore," grinned Hogg-Marchmont. "The

house is rebuilding itself, and its former inhabitants are now returning, one by one. Hogg Hall is playing with time."

"God, I love this place," bellowed Melton, and he made a beeline for the claret.

When Hardy told Lazarus Egg what year it was, he took it pretty well. Although an educated man, he had no concept of the space-time continuum so had little choice but to accept the fact that he had somehow travelled into the early twenty-first century at the command of a stately home.

"What happened to the East Wing?" he asked Hogg-Marchmont.

"It fell down," replied the Sixth Earl, "but I have a feeling that it'll be back soon."

Lazarus Egg took a tour of the stable block, and it was the same as when he set out for his fateful ride in 1791, a year that to him seemed little more than a few hours ago. Egg's room was on the First floor of the stables, on the east-facing aspect, and when he returned to it, it was exactly as he had left it that morning. He looked out of the window. There were many things in the grounds of Hogg Hall that he'd never seen before, the Sixth Earl's observatory, for example, and the defensive moat that now encircled the house. His eye was particularly drawn to Hardy's dented Daimler which was parked on the gravel drive. He could not see how to harness a stag to this unusual-shaped carriage, but he was sure he would figure it out.

Next day, Lazarus headed for the heather moorlands, a leather bridle slung over his shoulder and a riding crop in his hand. He was disappointed to discover that the sapphire stag herd was now a fraction of the size it had been in the eighteenth century. He moved slowly towards a huge male who was making a tasty meal of some fallen elderberries and twigs. The stag eyed him suspiciously, but it did not run away. Lazarus picked up a handful of acorns and gently offered them to the beast. The stag ate from his hand, and a quarter of a century melted away. Lazarus stroked the stag's hind quarters and, after a few minutes of calm grooming, he chose his moment to throw the harness around the animal's neck and leap onto its back. The stag reared up and tried to throw the rider onto the hard ground, but Lazarus Egg had done this too many times to be so easily dislodged. The creature's giant antlers thrust backwards in an effort to stab the stag's unwelcome passenger, but Egg grabbed hold of them like handlebars, and the animal took off at a full gallop.

By the end of the week, there were four magnificent sapphire stags in the stables at Hogg Hall.

"I shall call mine Lancelot," said Melton Thornaby, as he admired the largest and oldest of the three creatures.

"You'll never get on that thing's back in a million years," sneered Ingleby-Barwick.

"I'll have you know that I am a very fine horseman!" insisted Melton, even as he realised that horsemen ride horses not stags.

"I'll wager," said Hardy, "that Thornaby will stay on his mount for at least thirty seconds before the blasted thing throws him off and tramples him to death."

"The stags will not harm you," assured Lazarus Egg. "They are ancestors of the original Hogg-Marchmont herd, and they know it is their destiny to serve their masters at Hogg Hall."

"I wish I shared your optimism," said Ingleby-Barwick. "They still look pretty wild to me."

Hardy eyed the sleekest and most powerful-looking stag. "I shall call mine Excalibur," he said.

Lazarus Egg threw a saddle onto Excalibur's back, and the stag flinched a little. He made eye contact with Hardy and snorted.

"Are you ready?" Lazarus asked Hardy.

"Oh dear, oh dear," replied the Sixth Earl, "I can see you have much to learn about how we set about things around here."

Melton laughed. "Oh, yes, we couldn't possibly go riding without having a little livener first."

By 'little livener', Melton of course meant that he and his companions would first go to the Pig & Pencil Case and drink enough ale to sink the *Bismark*.

"Very well," replied Lazarus. He did, of course, understand. He had worked for this family for a very long time.

Hogg-Marchmont, like his ancestors before him, considered that getting drunk before going riding made the whole exercise a lot less dangerous. It reduced one's anxiety, removed inhibitions, and if you fell off, you hit the ground in a much more relaxed fashion and were less likely to hurt yourself. Man and boy, Melton Thornaby had never mounted anything sober, and he was not planning to start now.

"These days we get pissed purely for health and safety," Hardy explained to Lazarus Egg, and he, Melton and Angus headed towards the pub.

"Won't you join us?" Ingleby-Barwick called out to their riding instructor, but Lazarus politely declined. Some things had changed little since the days of the First Earl. Three hours later, their bellies full of beer, Hardy, Angus and Melton could be found desperately hanging onto the reigns of their sapphire stags as they galloped at full pelt across the heather moorlands. Lazarus Egg did his best to lead them by the safest path, but none of the men were fully in control of their animal, and there was a worrying randomness about the route they were taking. At one point, Melton rode so close to the edge of the cliffs that Lazarus was certain that both he and his stag were going to plunge onto the jagged rocks below, and the Sixth Earl narrowly avoided colliding with overhanging branches on numerous occasions. Had he made contact, it's anyone's guess what century he would have woken up in.

The trio were about to turn for home, when Ingleby-Barwick spotted a fox.

"Tally-ho!" he cried.

"Lord protect us," Lazarus Egg muttered under his breath, and Hardy and his companions took off in pursuit of the terrified little creature. Just as Lazarus had predicted, the stags seemed to know instinctively how to hunt with a saddle on their back, but he wasn't worried about the stags; he was worried about the safety of his masters. Ingleby-Barwick had named his stag Shirley, even though it was male, and as the animal accelerated after the fox, he was clearly having trouble holding on. Melton Thornaby was bouncing up and down in the saddle as if he was on a trampoline, and every now and then he would let go of one of the reigns to take a sip from a half bottle of Rémy

Martin cognac, which he had tucked into the top of his riding breeches.

"Hold on, man!" screamed Lazarus Egg, but Melton was having way too much fun to take any notice. Hardy was leaning forward as if he was riding a motorbike and had hold of his stag's antlers like handlebars. The beast seemed a little irritated by this, and he would occasionally flick his head mischievously in order to try and loosen Hogg-Marchmont's grip. This would be a hunt to end all hunts and a tale that would be told in the snug bar of the Pig & Pencil Case for many years to come.

*

It was a Sunday afternoon, and at Muddleton's tiny parish church, there was a service in progress. There was a good turnout that day, and Mrs. Snelling had just finished playing 'All Things Bright and Beautiful' on the recently restored pipe organ. The Reverend Ian Pardew, fresh-faced, earnest and relatively new to the parish, made his way to the lectern and opened a richly adorned Bible, inside of which he had secreted a neatly typed page containing his sermon.

"If we do good things," he began, "then good things will happen."

Jesus, Joseph and Mary looked down from the beautiful, priceless fifteenth-century stained-glass window above the alter. Mrs. Snelling closed the lid of the organ a little too loudly and whispered, "Sorry," to the congregation.

The vicar went on. "If we do good things, then we will be rewarded, and the Lord himself, in all his glory, will come to Muddleton. Maybe the Lord will come next week; maybe the Lord will come tomorrow; or maybe he is going to come through those very doors in the next few seconds."

Everyone turned around to look at the arched, oaken doors of the church. A small boy giggled. Nothing happened for two seconds, and then the doors were smashed open by a pair of stag's antlers, onto which were clamped the hands of Hardy Hogg-Marchmont, Sixth Earl of Hogg Hall.

"I can't stop the fucking thing!" he screamed at the top of his voice, and the stag galloped along the central aisle of the church towards the alter.

As the congregation screamed in panic, two more giant stags, ridden by Melton and Ingleby-Barwick, came crashing into the chapel. Thornaby's mount, spooked by a slightly creepy statue of the Virgin Mary, tried to turn 180 degrees, and in doing so, trampled over nine or ten wooden pews, some of which had terrified parishioners hiding underneath them, and one of which concealed a fox. Angus's stag, disquieted by its unfamiliar surroundings, began using its antlers to fiercely attack a finely carved effigy of St. Francis of Assisi. Observing this desecration of church property, and aghast at the sight of a black man in a toga on the back of a stag, the Reverend Pardew sprang to the defence of the saint by swinging wildly at both creature and jockey with a heavy brass crucifix.

"Fuck! Fuck! Fuck!" yelled Hardy, as his stag launched itself from the stone floor and, like a National Hunt runner, cleared the alter in a single bound. Unable to stop when it landed on the other side, it took off again and this time smashed clean through the stained-glass window, sending little shards of coloured glass and lead in all directions.

Not wishing to be outdone by Hardy's stag, the other two beasts followed in his footsteps, and both of them, one after the other, hurdled over the alter and leapt through the gaping hole in the stained glass. Whereas the first stag had managed to clear the candles on the alter, the second and third were not so lucky, and they both knocked over burning candles as they hurtled past.

At that moment, Lazarus Egg, on his own mount, appeared in the doorway. He quickly surveyed the damage before skilfully turning his stag away and galloping off in the general direction of Hogg Hall. The sound of sobbing and shouting came from inside the church, as Hogg-Marchmont, Melton and Angus finally got their stags under control and managed to pull them to a halt in the graveyard.

"Well, I think that went rather well," said Hardy.

"Where's Lazarus Egg?" asked Ingleby-Barwick.

"Can't take the pace," said Melton.

The familiar sound of approaching police sirens filled the air, and the trio clambered off their stags and made their escape down a steep and narrow alleyway than ran down the side of the church and came out near the harbour.

"Exhilarating!" panted Hardy as they ran, and he glimpsed over his shoulder to see that the entire church was now fully ablaze.

That night, as he slowly sobered up and began to feel a little guilty about the fire at the church, Hardy sat on the swing seat next to the observatory and stared at Hogg Hall. A voice came from behind him.

"It's not going to repair itself while you're watching," said the voice. Hardy turned around, and Celestia May was standing behind him.

"It'll happen when you least expect it," she said, "while you're not looking. When you're not even thinking about it."

Hardy looked away, counted to ten, then looked back, but the East Wing was still missing.

"How do you know all these things?" the Sixth Earl asked his daughter.

"The house speaks to me," she said.

"What's it saying now?" asked Hardy.

"Nothing," whispered Celestia May, "the house is asleep."

Epilogue

The chronicles of Hogg Hall have been painstakingly assembled by studying thousands of documents, papers, ledgers and diaries stored on the dusty shelves of the Great Library. However, down through the centuries, the six Earls proved to be remarkably incompetent when it came to keeping records and writing things down. Subsequently, many of these documents have been either lost, misfiled or deliberately destroyed, in case they should be used in evidence.

We can, however, now clear up one mystery which has puzzled the Hogg-Marchmont family for some time, and that is the matter of precisely how Hardy Hogg-Marchmont managed to convincingly fake his own death. You might remember that it was the last day of the not entirely legal Muddleton Christmas Hunt. Hardy was riding his favourite horse Old Trotter, and he apparently met his maker after a particularly nasty fall in the north woods.

When Hardy turned up at Hogg Hall, soon after his own funeral, all he would say was that the subterfuge had been achieved using the services of 'a man with a van', and no amount of prompting would tempt him to reveal any further details.

Ingleby-Barwick having stumbled upon one of Hogg-Marchmont's secret diaries in the observatory, we are now able to reveal precisely what happened on that fateful day. It seems that as the hunt turned southwards, close to the Great Henry Oak, Hardy deliberately dropped back to the rear of the riding party and he and his horse slipped behind a large holly bush. The Sixth Earl quietly climbed off his mount, and after dabbing a generous amount of pig's blood over his face, he lay on the ground and waited. Ten minutes later, Melton Thornaby, who due to his considerable additional weight, always rode near the back of the pack, noticed that Hardy was missing. He cantered back into the woods to look for him, only stopping six or seven times to take swigs of Balvenie single malt from his hip flask. By the time Thornaby reached the apparently stricken and blood-covered Hogg-Marchmont, the Sixth Earl was already being loaded into the back of an ambulance by two luminously clad paramedics. The vehicle had disappeared out of sight by the time Melton clambered off his horse and surveyed the scene of the accident. Thornaby was far too drunk to wonder who had called an ambulance and how it had reached the middle of the north woods so quickly.

An hour later, the family arrived at Muddleton Cottage Hospital to be immediately told that the Sixth Earl had been 'dead on arrival'. When the doctor asked Countess Isabella if she, or any of the other family members, would like to see his body, she said no.

Needless to say, the ambulance was hired from a film props company; the paramedics were two recent graduates of the Royal Central School of Speech and Drama; and the dead body that was delivered to the hospital, wearing Hardy's fox hunter jacket, had been supplied by the Sixth Earl's mysterious 'man with a van'.

We can now reveal that this man was Alessandro Alessandro, godfather to Hardy's daughter Lady Celestia May and a card-carrying member of the Cosa Nostra.

But, you are probably thinking, *what if Countess Isabella or another family member had said they wanted to see the body?*

While planning this elaborate deception, Hardy had given this much thought, and he was fairly certain that this would not be the case. Ever squeamish about such things, his wife had not even wanted to see the body of her own father after he passed away, so the Sixth Earl was fairly certain that she would not want to see his own blood-splattered remains. Indeed, the Countess was generally not that keen on looking at Hardy, even when he was alive.

As a contingency plan, the body that Alessandro Alessandro supplied to Muddleton hospital actually bore a striking resemblance to Hardy. It was the body of a man called Daniel Glebe and had been painstakingly selected from the pages of actors' Spotlight, which Alessandro borrowed from the office of a friend who was a film director.

Hardy knew that the only person curious enough to want to look at him on a slab would be his old friend Thornaby, and he was sure that on the last day of the

Christmas hunt, his friend would be far too drunk to notice if the body was that of a lookalike.

Daniel Glebe was not Daniel Glebe's real name. It was his stage name. He'd been an actor for over thirty years and, in all that time, had only secured one paid acting role: that of the vicar in a Whitehall farce called *See How They Run*. He had received extremely poor reviews.

It was Daniel Glebe who Alessandro Alessandro went and sat next to in the Blue Posts pub in Berwick Street. It was Daniel Glebe the Mafia man got drunk and later quietly suffocated with a plastic carrier bag from Sainsbury's. It was Daniel Glebe whose body was burnt at Muddleton Crematorium, and it was Daniel Glebe's ashes that were now scattered in a peaceful spot next to the lake at Hogg Hall. Daniel Glebe played the part of Hardy Hogg-Marchmont brilliantly, but he received no reviews for doing it.

It's also now well documented that, before putting this plan into practice, Hardy had forgotten to check to see if his life insurance policy was fully paid up. As a result, Hogg Hall received none of the funds it so urgently needed, and Daniel Glebe died in vain.